ALIZEL'S Song

BILL POTTLE

Ellechor Publishing House, LLC

Copyright ©2012 Bill Pottle
2013 Ellechor Publishing House Edition

Alizel's Song/ Pottle, Bill
ISBN: 9781937844882
Library of Congress Control Number: 2012953187

Ellechor Publishing House
1915 NW Amberglen Parkway, Suite 400
Beaverton, OR 97006

Cover & Interior Design by ZAQ Designs
Printed in the United States of America

www.ellechorpublishing.com

Fr. Marty,

Thanks so much for everything. You have really been a blessing to our parish and our family. We wish you all the best in your new parish and will miss you tremendously here at QOP.

To Michael, may you always watch over us.

4/21/13

Author's Note

I've always loved a great story. There was something about the sacrifice of the hero, the tyranny of the villain, and the triumph when all seemed lost. I've loved listening to them as a child and loved writing them as an adult.

The Bible has been called "*The greatest story ever told.*" In a lot of ways, however, it's The Story. For Christians, it's really the only story that matters. The Story has everything that matters in a good story, and one critical thing more. It's the only Story that you can go inside of. There was always a twinge of sadness whenever I read about a sunset in a made up world— knowing that I could never, really, be a part of that story.

As an author, I wish that I could claim to have written this Story, but most of The Story was written long before I was born. What I have tried to do is give a different perspective on it based on what we know about the world. Some people who give the Bible no more than a quick glance will dismiss it out of hand because of apparent contradictions. They ignore the only way human knowledge increases, by using our current understanding to its limits, and then finding new theories to resolve the apparent contradictions by tying everything together.

The split between science and religion is a modern phenomenon. It used to just be called "knowledge." This book tries to use new ideas to heal the split between two different ways of looking at the world. The central question of the work is: could they both be right? Could they be just two ways of looking at the same Truth? Could the Works of God in nature give us a lens through which to understand the Works of God in scripture?

If I've added anything, it's a way to look at the unanswered questions. Science and religion both have holes in our understanding of the Universe. The Bible gives us many stories, but leaves out many others. What happened in the generations where only a name was mentioned? What did Jesus do from 12 to 30? When He was a carpenter, how did He feel each time His hammer hit a nail?

Science gives us many tools to explore the Universe, and helps to understand much of the 'what' as well as the 'immediate why.' Yet it cannot provide an answer to the 'ultimate why.' We know that if any of several fundamental constants were off by less than one part in a million, life as we know if would not be able to exist. Does this suggest design, or rather the fact that if everything wasn't perfect, we would simply not exist and therefore not notice?

Looking at science and religion together can bring interesting and surprising insights. For example, the scriptures often talk about the battle between Good and Evil as akin to that between light and darkness. Many people mistakenly take light and darkness to be opposites when that is not, in fact, their relationship. It is in the nature of light to always, and immediately, conquer darkness. Thus there can be no real 'battle' between the two. It is a one way relationship. Light can go where there is darkness, and the darkness is dispelled literally as quickly as possible (at the speed of light.) Yet darkness cannot go where light is and act similarly.

How then, can darkness hope to battle light? Darkness spreads only by blocking light (absorbing the photons), or by destroying sources of light. Therefore a reasonable strategy for Satan would be to try to do everything possible to disrupt Man's relationship with God. Satan cannot try to confront God directly, as that would lead to his instant annihilation.

Studying science and scripture, I see a number of cases where a scripture made sense to our ancestors who were first hearing it, and yet makes a different kind of sense as our scientific knowledge about the world increases. It's hard for modern humans to imagine a time without electric lights, yet when we are camping and our fire is the only light for miles, we can get a glimpse into the soul of a previous time, and know how important that light must have seemed to ancient peoples. They understood these verses viscerally in a way that we do not. Yet, we understand them intellectually in a way that they never could. How could something be so simple, yet so profound?

PART ONE

"In the beginning God created the heavens and the earth."
-Genesis 1:1

At least, that's how they would describe it fifteen billion years later. Shortly after that— so soon, in fact, that it was almost no time at all, they'd call it the "Big Bang." It was quite an odd name, for it was neither big— at least not until 10^{-37} seconds after it started— nor a bang, for this was long before the formation of even the simplest element, let alone air. Without air, there was no sound, and certainly no bangs.

But that's how humans worked. Things had to be explained in ways that they could understand. Try to let one see too far and the door to their mind would slam shut in your face. It was like trying to teach a rock to jump. The mentality just wasn't there. This rule couldn't ever be broken for any human, even for Him.

I wasn't about to question God, for if there's one thing I've learned through all of this it's that His plans far outweigh what even we angels can see. Every time we thought we had figured out something fundamental, He always sprung a surprise on us. I'd be talking from a very different place right now if I hadn't learned to trust Him from the beginning.

I'm not vain enough to fool myself: you're not really interested in my story. You've probably never even heard of the name of Alizel. But I know the story that you want to hear. I know it because I was there— not always on the front lines, but lurking behind the scenes. Now I could tell you only what I saw firsthand, but who wants a story full of a bunch of 'he saids' and 'she saids?' The main events that happened are the stuff of legends up here. Every conversation, battle, or piece of trickery has been told and retold a thousand times over. So if you don't mind, I'll tell what

I wasn't there for the same as if I were. My information came only from reliable sources, and as we angels are good at sharing our memories when we want to, I think I got a pretty good picture of what happened.

This is my story.

CHAPTER ONE:

THE BEGINNING

Alizel watched it, uncertain of what it could mean. Uriel the Principality was on his left, his soft brown eyes and brown shoulder length hair in sharp contrast to his earthy green wings. Uriel's lips pushed together and his wings gave a slight flutter. It was obvious that he didn't know any more than Alizel.

Verin was standing on Alizel's right, his golden sash bunched up as he placed his forearms on the railing. The white V on the sash didn't stand for his name, but rather signified the rank of Virtue. His flaming red hair shot out from his head at all angles, and his sea-green wings seemed always ready to explode out and head off to the next adventure. Alizel could tell from his expression that Verin wanted very much to know what was going on, but he didn't know any more than anyone else.

They were at the Portal, the place where the Realm of Spirit intersected with the newly created Realm of Matter. The Portal was a shimmering pool, unconnected with any of the waterways of Heaven, surrounded by a metallic railing that signified the farthest point that angels could go before they risked entering the Realm of Matter. Angels could look through its surface and gaze upon the Realm of Matter, which at this point, was just a small mass. The mass was expanding outward, moving steadily, homogenous as far as they could see, and in reality, not all that interesting.

It had been going on like that for a few minutes. Alizel knew it was important, from the conversations he had he knew that much had been felt by everyone from the lowest Unranked to the highest Seraph. They could feel in His Will that this was an important event, but it was hard to imagine something like this being more important than the latest events in Heaven.

"What do you think it is? It looks like another world."

"I don't understand why He needed to create another world," Verin said, leaning over the rail to look closer. "What's wrong with this one?"

"Who's to say He's going to stop at one," Uriel spoke up. "Maybe He's making a hundred, or a thousand?"

The angels had been enjoying their newfound existence for only a short time, each of them had been created in an instant, fully formed and in awe of the Lord God who had created them and Heaven.

"Maybe He just made ours first because it's the best," Verin answered, lines of worry creasing his otherwise handsome face.

"Maybe you should stop questioning His motives."

The voice coming from behind them was light and strong, radiant as a silver mirror reflecting the Father's glory.

They whirled, apologizing. The figure behind them was tall and sleek, crimson wings bursting from his shoulder blades, aerodynamic and smooth. His cloak was brilliant white, and the fiery S emblazoned on the sash across his shoulder matched perfectly with the color and quality of his eyes. He was tall, yet his long, platinum hair still reached his waist. Not a strand was ever out of place.

"I'm sorry, sir." Alizel managed to get his apology out first. "But we just don't know what's required of us. We are all so very new."

"Trust in God is all that's required. The rest will be revealed— even to you— when the time is right."

With that he smiled and walked away.

When he was safely out of hearing distance, Verin parodied his expression. "'Even to you.' Those Seraphim think they know everything. What's his name again?"

"Luciferel." Uriel answered quickly.

"He probably doesn't even know. He just acts like that because he's so highly ranked. I bet he wouldn't talk to a Cherub like that."

Alizel didn't bother to answer him. He just kept staring at the sphere as it continued expanding outwards into nothingness and creating space for itself. It had cooled significantly in the first few minutes, but he still couldn't imagine what it would become. They watched it and tossed around theories for a few more hours before shrugging it off and walking away.

Alizel sat down on a perfectly shaped stone on the banks of one of the smaller streams, letting his white wings slide down into the water and feeling the passing liquid tickle and caress his feathers. He thought nothing of taking a moment for introspection — he had no reason to believe that he had anything other than an infinite amount of time. And besides, this was one of his favorite spots.

There were no houses in Heaven, a place needed for safety and rest. Heaven *was* safety, at the same time both alive and yet so tranquil. There was no need for walls to keep out strangers, and all Heaven was home. In Heaven there was no need of rest, for angels' bodies continually received energy from the glory of the Father. They did not grow weary or have any desire to stop. Every moment Alizel was bursting with the energy of a thousand possibilities. Rest was not something that he yearned for.

If an angel wanted to, he could find privacy in one of the common rooms or fellowship in one of the thousands of larger buildings designed for groups of angels to relax in easy conversation or praise. The buildings were generally curved so that all of the assembled angels could speak together and yet still gaze upon the Father. No wall could stop His sustaining energy from reaching them, but when given a choice, the angels always preferred to gaze upon Him. The buildings curved as amphitheaters with openings toward Mt. Zion, so that there could be an unobstructed view of the One who was their reason for being.

Alizel spent most of his time praising God, not out of obligation but love. Angels were free to praise the Father privately at any time, and often did so. Yet nothing was more beautiful than when the entire assembled host burst forth into praise at once. Sometimes it was scheduled under the conducting of the Cherub Jehudiel, and sometimes it was spontaneous, but compelling either way. If he heard angels around him begin to sing, then Alizel wanted nothing more than to join in.

How to describe the sound — the purity of each voice, the melody of hundreds of thousands together, the power of the song that roared forth like a tsunami, yet held the gentleness of a single flower petal…. It was a song sung not with the lips but the soul.

Alizel and his friends spent time in nearly every corner of Heaven. They danced in the meadows, swam in the rivers, lounged in the treetops, and sometimes just soared over everything, gliding effortlessly and taking it all in. Pretty much the only place they didn't go was the throne room of God. Although they worshiped the Lord without ceasing and loved him dearly, sometimes His love for them was almost too strong. Feeling such beauty concentrated into a single room was too much for even an ordinary angel. It seemed only the Cherubim and Seraphim could stand such intensity. Those two orders of angels weren't like the rest of them. Seraphim seemed more 'normal,' almost as if they were just a better version of the other ranks of angels. Cherubim, on the other hand…well, it was almost as if they were a completely different species.

All of the ranks did spend a great deal of time at the Portal, just looking at the Realm of Matter. As it expanded it became more interesting, if only for its differences with Heaven. They took to calling the Realm of Matter "the Universe." It had a completely different set of physical laws than Heaven. It had one energy like Heaven, but that energy could take many forms. It was the attraction of gravity, and the attraction charge between positive and negative, between matter and antimatter. The energy could be stored as matter or released with the splitting or fusing of tiny particles. Heaven's one energy, though, only had one form. The Father himself radiated out all that the angels needed to survive. It was food, drink, sleep, light, purpose, and love. Alizel and indeed every other angel craved it, yet were satisfied at every moment. It was the water of eternal life.

One thing that angels did have in common with the Universe was time. Angels didn't age— they learned from the past, and increased in wisdom, but their bodies stayed the same.

At least… that was true for most angels.

Alizel and his friends were able to watch time passing in that other world, often going down to the Portal to watch it for years in one sitting.

They were always disappointed.

"Is it just going to stay like that forever?" Verin blurted out once, leaning over the railing. "If God created our world in an instant, why is this one taking so long?"

Verin was a good friend, but he never seemed satisfied. Alizel wasn't sure how, but Verin's curiosity was different than their friend, Mupiel's. Mupiel was a blond Unranked angel who questioned everything, always wanting to know why everything happened. Verin always seemed like he needed to *make* something happen.

"Perhaps it's supposed to stay that way," Alizel offered, shrugging his shoulders.

"Oh, yes," Verin replied, sweeping his hand around at the bright columns, flowing streams, and fiery energy that was home. "God who could make this beauty has nothing better to do than to make a big cloud of particles."

Alizel had to admit that he did have a point. It didn't make much sense. "Well, some of them are sticking together," Alizel noticed, pointing. Although angels couldn't speed up or slow down time in the new world, they could zoom in or out, seeing the entirety or the insides of the small particles made up of other smaller particles.

"Hallelujah!" Verin cried out, voice dripping with sarcasm. "That world so far exceeds ours that I might as well leave home and fly down there!"

He stood up on the edge of the pool, a slow, smooth grin coming to his face as he looked down on it. He looked around to see if it was safe. No one else was around. "I'm sure it wouldn't hurt…"

Before Alizel could stop him, Verin shot up into the air, streamlining his body and raising his green wings for the flap that would propel him into a nosedive across the shining surface of the barrier.

A golden and platinum streak arced out of nowhere and slammed into Verin's body as his wings were in mid flap. The streak hurtled him to the ground and pinned him under the golden armor.

"What do you think you are doing?" the Power bellowed at him. "You know entering the Realm of Matter is forbidden!"

"How… dare you touch me," Verin stammered, shaking to get the words out. "I'm a Virtue." It was true; technically he was more highly ranked than the Power sitting on top of him. "Besides, I thought we were to go there."

Azazel's armor dug into his chest. Verin winced.

"I bow to no rank. As the guardian of Heaven, I am free to challenge any who dares set foot in the Universe."

Alizel cringed for his friend. Of all the angels to run afoul of, Verin had to pick this one. Azazel was not someone to get on your bad side. He was head of the Powers, the group of angels that guarded the borders of Heaven. They all wore armor and red sashes with a platinum P emblazoned over their shoulders. With the way that they carried themselves, a piece of cloth denoting their rank was unnecessary.

Up to this point, Heaven had never been under attack, but apparently they even needed to be protected from themselves.

"We are to go there," Azazel informed, although by the tone of his voice it was obvious that he had not bought Verin's excuse and did not really respect his authority. "But the time is not yet. The world is too young."

He still had not relaxed his hold on Verin's body.

"Do you have any idea what would happen if you went there now?" Azazel growled.

Verin shook his head. "I thought we couldn't really change that world. Just in the tiniest ways."

Azazel's silver eyes hardened. "It's too early. Even quantum changes now could throw the entire plan off course."

He sat up, finally relaxing his grip on the Virtue. "Do you want that? Do you want to destroy everything God has worked to make?"

"No… no, sir. I'm sorry, sir. It won't happen again."

"Be sure that it doesn't." Azazel got up and straightened out his robes under his shining armor. "Next time I will not be so forgiving."

Then he was gone, almost as quickly as he had arrived. The gardens were bright, the streams flowed and swirled, and peace was in the air. Except for Verin cowering on the ground next to the pool, it was like the whole incident never happened.

Verin put his palm to the ground and pushed himself up to his knees, visibly shaken. He turned to Alizel and raised his eyes without speaking.

Azazel had been so fast, so sure. If there ever were any threats, Alizel felt confident with him leading the defense of Heaven. Alizel shrugged. "At least it looks like they got the right angel for the job."

Flying high above the majesty of Heaven, Alizel reflected back on how Azazel was responsible for leading the defense of the Realm of Spirit. Only a few angels had jobs. Most were like Alizel, unranked with no profession. It was a bit unsettling at times, wondering about his place. With some of the other orders, everything seemed so clear for them. They knew what they were made for. Alizel had always felt like he had some purpose in life, but just couldn't figure out what it was. If any of the higher ones knew, they were keeping silent.

They all answered to the Seraphim, the 'flaming ones.' Alizel didn't see them very often, and didn't really have any clue what they did. Secretive and powerful, they very rarely spent any time with lower ranking angels at all. There were very few Seraphim and it was impossible to mistake them for any other order. They wore their platinum sashes with a crimson S more for pride than for identification. Luciferel was the leader of the Seraphim, and by extension leader of all angels. There had been no election or word from God to confirm his leadership, but it just didn't seem right that it could be any other way.

The Cherubim were technically next in rank, although sometimes Alizel wondered why they weren't the highest. They were the most knowledgeable, and some said they completely knew the mind of God. Alizel wasn't so sure, though. If he ever had a question, they were the ones to go to— if they'd ever agree to talk to him. They seemed genuinely uninterested in the daily life of Heaven and the affairs of its inhabitants. The joke was that it was easy to identify a member of the Cherubim: just look for their white sashes with a golden C…and their four faces and wings.

Following them were the Thrones. Alizel didn't see much of them either. There were only twelve of them, but Thrones was just a name. He had heard that they had a special task, far above the other angels, but after asking and asking Alizel couldn't get any closer to it. Mupiel had of course been asking about as well, and no one would tell him either. Their task was a great secret, and Alizel wondered if anyone who was not a Throne knew what it was. At times they looked like the other angels, and at times nothing like them. Sometimes they appeared as two concentric fiery wheels, with eyes everywhere along the rims. Even in a form like the other angels, they still had multiple eyes. Alizel guessed that's why they always knew so much – they could see everything. The Thrones wore earthy brown sashes with a green T and served as instructors to the other angels.

The fourth order was the Dominions. They never seemed to fit. It was obvious to all that they had some job as they strutted around in their long white albs, purple sashes with a golden D, and their golden belts. The huge buckles had strange shapes on them, shapes like nothing seen in Heaven. They were always off doing their own thing—probably trying to find what their purpose was, Alizel reasoned.

After the Dominions came the Virtues, resplendent in their white albs and golden sashes with a white V. They didn't know what their job was either, but at least they were honest enough to admit it. Verin, of course, was the most impatient to discover his purpose.

Next were the Powers, with Azazel as their chief. They were the gatekeepers who kept the separation between the worlds fixed. They were always so aloof, standing there in their golden armor and red sashes. Alizel wasn't ashamed to admit that sometimes the Powers scared him, even more so after the incident with Verin and the Portal.

The lower angels had three ranks of their own. There were the Principalities, whose job it was to watch over a hundred angels, Archangels who watched over ten, and the majority like Alizel, the Unranked. Principalities wore white sashes with a blue P on them, Archangels wore white sashes with a green letter A, and the Unranked wore grey sashes with no letter at all.

Uriel was Alizel's Principality. Though he watched over a hundred angels, Alizel always felt that he was closer to him than the others. He was like a mentor. No—he *was* a mentor, at least more than Katel, his Archangel. It wasn't that Alizel had any problems with Katel, a lithe creature whose purple wings seemed even more colorful next to his short black hair. On the contrary, they had always got along well. It was just that Katel's indigo eyes always seemed to stop their search just short of something really worth seeing. But was being satisfied with a perfect life really so wrong?

The ranking of the angels was set in stone from the moment of creation, and Alizel often meditated on the different orders of angels and what it might mean. Why were the Powers, who were so strong, near the bottom? They seemed like the closest to the Seraphim in strength and might. He could understand why the Powers weren't higher than the Cherubim, but did ranking so low mean that protecting Heaven was unimportant? What jobs did the other angels have? And would they ever learn the secret of the Thrones?

Chapter Two:

The Weapon

Alizel often thought back fondly on those early years. If humans knew of the time angels spent then, their hearts would burst from the pure joy of it. There was unimaginable happiness for billions of years on end. If every tree on Earth was cut down there wouldn't be enough paper to print the books he could fill with the stories of that time.

It's hard to know when anything really began. Things began in the deepest recesses of the soul. But if he was going to try to trace it back, he had to start with one particular event. There was one meeting of the Angelarch that always stood out in Alizel's mind later.

Governing was easier than it looked. Angels didn't have to worry about being provided with food, water, or shelter since their bodies were completely fueled by the radiant energy from the Father. They never had to worry about sleeping, eating, or disease, and contentious debates never occurred because everyone shared everything else.

The major decisions were made by a meeting of the Angelarch. The entire assembly of Heaven met together in the stadium to gather and debate, sometimes for days. Voting was done by will alone, with respect to each angel's rank. Each Unranked got one vote and it continued up the hierarchy with each Seraph getting nine. Even though each Unranked only got one vote, there were so many that as a whole they counted more than anyone.

The Father didn't participate in the discussions, although He did maintain veto power over any vote. Angels were all tied directly to His Will, and knew when something was contrary to it.

There was a memorable meeting shortly after Verin's attempted trespass. Azazel had summoned it. It was quite bold. Seraphim and Cherubim were the ones that usually called for the meetings, although occasionally a Throne would make a demand to meet. Yet since he was the head of the Powers and in charge of the defense of Heaven, Azazel's word held a lot of sway. His reputation for being a serious, capable commander who didn't put up with nonsense added to his influence.

Angels generally sat by rank, with six sections for the upper six ranks. However, higher ranking angels could sit in the sections reserved for lower ranks if they wished to attend the meetings with their friends. The Cherubim section was usually half empty as they rarely left God's side. The rest sat in the largest section, organized by the tens and hundreds with Archangels and Principalities sitting among their groups. There was no need for amplified sound. If one wished to address the assembly, he simply stood and began talking in a normal voice and all heard him clearly.

The stadium was in a "U" shape with the open end facing towards Mt. Zion and the Throne of God, that way the radiant energy of the Father could flow through the meetings and no angel there would turn his back on God. The top section of the stadium made a natural curve along the rim of the "U". Each raised section was held in the air without the need for any supporting columns or flying buttresses, and the seats were L-shaped blocks of cool white marble which provided back support while letting the angels' wings hang free.

"What do you think he's going to say?" Alizel turned at Abbadon's voice.

Abbadon was a Virtue with silver wings and blood-red hair. His features were darker and he wore robes of white and black under the gold sash.

"Well, I…"

"I don't care," Verin interrupted from beside Abbadon. "I just wish they would get this meeting started already so we can get back to our business."

"You don't have any business," Abbadon reminded him curtly. "None of us do. Ten billion years later and we still don't have a mission."

"You're just nervous to see Azazel," Abbadon joked. "Worried he might jump on you again."

"I'm not afraid of him." Verin stuck out his chest. A faint shiver passed through his body and fluttered his green wings.

"I find that hardly convincing," Abbadon smirked and sat back into his seat, running a hand through his dark hair.

"Besides, we're *supposed* to be afraid of Azazel," Alizel reminded. "That's why he's in charge of protecting us."

Verin was about to reply when Azazel himself stood. He looked even more imposing than before, his golden armor polished until it shone radiantly. He was wearing the full formal breastplate, gauntlets, and shin protectors, and carried his crimson-plumed helmet in the crook of his arm so that his blond hair spilled out over his shoulders. His sharp platinum wings unfurled behind him to make him, if possible, even more imposing.

"Inhabitants of Heaven— noble Seraphim, wise Cherubim, steadfast Thrones, loyal Dominions, pure Virtues, fellow Powers, watchful Principalities, blessed Archangels, and Unranked." He paused to take a breath after he finished with the full ceremonial list. "You know that from the beginning, my fellow Powers and I have been untiring in our duty of protecting the borders of Heaven."

At this a polite clap issued forth from the crowd. The Powers had certainly done well, although there was nothing that could challenge them. Alizel glanced over his shoulder and noticed Verin was the only angel not applauding.

"We were created for this purpose, and for this purpose alone we owe our existence to Almighty God. We will continue in our duties, without relenting, into the far reaches of eternity!"

This earned him louder applause, and it was relieving to hear. This certainly wasn't a reason for calling together the full Angelarch, though.

"Yet, we can only protect you to the best of our abilities, with the tools and training we have received. We have undertaken an extensive study into the matter, and I am sad to report that we are missing a vital item."

Alizel's curiosity was piqued. What could he possibly need?

"As you are undoubtedly aware," he continued, "the Universe grows more complex by the day. We have already observed self-replicating localized zones of organization that can copy themselves over and over, and as time goes by, their complexity increases."

It was quite an exciting day when the angels had first discovered these primitive "cells." They were quite beautiful, Alizel thought. The planet Earth was the center of this action. Volcanic energy and sunlight caused groups of atoms to stick together in molecular building blocks, some of which had heads that were attracted to water, and tails repelled by it. These blocks arranged themselves in spheres with the heads on the outside. The amazing thing was that there was one molecule, the one humans would come to call RNA, that could both help the membranes organize themselves and help make more molecules like itself.

The angels didn't know it at the time, but that was the real turning point.

Azazel's voice rose. "Where will it all end? Who knows what these cells may continue to grow into? As molecules have self-organized into cells, what if the cells self-organize into larger organisms? What creatures may evolve on Earth, or other worlds? What if they move to challenge us and come to storm the gates of Heaven?"

A low murmuring rumbled through the Angelarch. Could it be true? Had God created the Universe as a home for other types of creatures?

Could Heaven be in danger?

"Yet these are not the only threats," he thundered on. "What if Heaven is threatened from within?"

Everyone fell silent. From within?

"Already there have been unauthorized attempts to go down to Earth. What if someone intentionally wanted to thwart God's plan? What if an angel were to sneak by us, and go to make his own mark on the world?"

A howl of protest rose up. "Preposterous!" cried several at once.

Alizel looked back at Verin again; his face had paled and he slumped deeper into his chair.

The Power held up his hands in defense. "I do not mean to call the good name of the assembled host into question, or accuse any specific angel. But there are more than a hundred thousand of us. It would be naive not to at least admit the possibility."

It suddenly seemed like everyone was talking at once.

The Seraph known as Michael held up his hands. "Enough!" he said, quieting the rest immediately. Fires danced in his eyes. Michael was second only to Luciferel. He had brilliant white feathers and short black hair, and his feathers were so sleek they almost seemed to slice the air when he flew. Michael was never without his special breastplate.

"What would you have us do, Azazel?"

Everyone waited.

Azazel took a breath, but his voice was strong and steady. "We need to ask the Father to make us a weapon."

There was a pause.

"What is a weapon?" a Virtue named Eleleth asked, rising from her seat. Alizel had always liked her. Soft, wise, and calm, she was one of the most important Virtues and an arbiter of conflict between others. Her golden hair was the exact color of the "V" on her white sash.

"Something powerful— an item that can end the existence of a being."

Silence. No one moved or spoke, the enormity of what he was asking pouring over the angels like a waterfall from Heaven's rivers. Such terms as "death" and "killing" were foreign to them. But they understood that this was something permanent.

Eleleth was the first to recover, although her voice was little more than a whisper. "Is such a thing even possible?"

"All is possible with God." Luciferel had been silent so far, but now he responded automatically.

A Seraph with brown hair and wings rose quietly. His name was Raphael, and Alizel always wondered if he really belonged to the highest order. He was always so calm and relaxed. If anything, Alizel felt safe with him. But as he looked at him now, Alizel wasn't so sure. Just because someone avoided conflict didn't mean that they wouldn't prevail at it. Raphael spoke softly, great concern in his voice. "But to destroy a being? Even an angel? What would happen to him?"

"That is not our concern, sir." Azazel's silver eyes were cold, hard. "Would you rather destroy one or risk the chance that we all could be annihilated if Heaven falls? The good of the whole must be paramount."

"We know not what we unleash," another voice spoke for the first time, but the angel remained seated, and Alizel craned his neck to see who was speaking. "How are we to know that this weapon will not fall into the wrong hands?" the voice went on. "This could be a greater threat to Heaven than anything to come from the Universe."

Gabriel was a Seraph whose council was sought by many. He was large, with ash blond curls and gray wings. He wore no armor, and Alizel wondered if it was due to his massive chest muscles being protection enough. Still, despite his size and obvious strength, he seemed to bow readily to the authority of Michael and Luciferel.

"This is true," Michael added. "The weapon being used for the wrong reasons would be a terrible threat. And even without this weapon, the Powers can hold the barrier between the worlds. Even if these cells on Earth become more complex, they may not be able to even reach the Kingdom."

"Azazel is not asking us to make such a weapon," Luciferel mused, his platinum hair falling gracefully over his ears. "He is only asking us to plead with God to do so. To me, this seems the obvious course. If the Lord does not think it a good idea, He will not forge the weapon."

This was a difficult point to argue. Still, those against the resolution would not be so easily swayed, and many were yet undecided.

Raphael spoke with a sadness in his voice. "It is up to God to choose whether or not to follow our requests, but that does not mean that He will be happy with us for making them. We have always enjoyed peace. Shall we risk giving it up now?"

"Sometimes violence is the price for peace." The dragon on his breastplate smiled as Michael spoke.

"There may be a compromise." The booming voice was from Orifel, head of the Thrones. Except for the head instructor Bodiel, it was rare to hear a Throne speak. When they spoke, they usually appeared like other angels…except with several sets of extra eyes all over their faces. Their concentric circle form didn't have a mouth, after all. Although they could communicate in other ways, using a mouth to speak was the most natural.

"There is a compromise," Orifel strengthened his statement. "It seems God, in His wisdom, has foreseen this."

His dramatic pause was not necessary. He had the full attention of every last angel present. How could there be a compromise between existing and not?

"Some time ago, He directed us Thrones to begin construction on a special repository. It is a chamber with one entrance and one exit. The chamber is nearing completion, and it was built so that its contents will be in a state of perpetual darkness, of existence without awareness."

"What is this new chamber to hold?" Raphael asked the question on everyone's minds. But it was odd, Alizel thought, for Raphael to be doing so. Didn't the Seraphim have privileged knowledge? Why was construction of a new part of Heaven told only to the Thrones?

"It is to hold the essence of an individual. It could hold an angel."

Eleleth was aghast. "This cannot be why it was ordered to be built? To contain angels?"

"Only the Father knows His purpose," Orifel responded, his multiple eyes blinking in acknowledgement. "But this seems an optimal solution to our concerns. The weapons Azazel desires could be made to send the essence of an angel to this trap. If the exit is sealed, they would remain there until it is safe for them to return."

Alizel leaned forward with his elbows on his knees, and thought about this compromise as he continued to watch the debate. The plan seemed like it had the potential to satisfy everyone. If an angel or other creature did somehow get out of hand, he could be sent to a place where he could no longer hurt himself or others. At the same time, nothing was permanent and he could always return later.

The debate continued for a few more hours, but the essential points had been laid on the table. In the end Azazel had his resolution, and the Father agreed. The Lord not only gave Azazel a weapon called a sword, but He taught him how to make his own.

A sword was a long, sharp piece of metal crossed with a smaller, blunt piece to protect one's hand. Below the smaller, blunt piece was a handle that ended in a pommel. The whole piece was infused with the energy of God by one of the Seraphim touching it to the Almighty Himself. This glory often made the sword flare up along the cutting edge.

Soon Azazel had forged swords for all of his Powers, and for many of the Seraphim as well. He offered to make some for the Cherubim, but they saw no need for them and declined. A passion for sword making seemed to consume Azazel, and he had an armory erected to store all of the weapons.

This dangerous power was not left unchecked, however. Angels were tasked to guard the armory, keeping perpetual watch. Each sword had to be signed out before use and signed in when the shift was over. Only Azazel kept his, as he rarely ever left his post. Some of the Seraphim had swords custom designed for them, and they wore them at all times as well.

Training in the weapons was open to all angels, although many were still unsure of the weapon's utility, and failed to take advantage of the opportunity. All training was done under heavy supervision by a higher ranking angel, usually a Power or Principality, and at the end of the session, all weapons were stored and locked away.

The angels all agreed that these sensible precautions would prevent any problem with misuse of the weapons.

They were all very wrong.

As part of Alizel's continuing education, the Throne Bodiel took him and his friends on flights, teaching them how to interact with the Universe. Alizel loved to fly and he loved to learn. The first time he had gone through the Portal to the Realm of Matter, he had been worried about what it would feel like. How would it be to be in a different realm from the Father? What if he couldn't feel God's Energy?

As it turned out, his worries were for nothing. They could still feel the Father. Although it was nothing like standing directly in God's presence, His love and energy still permeated the fabric of the Universe. Although not taking up any space while in the Universe, angels could "overlay" the Realm of Matter at any point. They could be at any point they wanted, yet since they had no matter they did not affect that world in any way.

Since the developments on Earth were so important, angels had started keeping track of time using Earth's measurement. Revolutions around the sun seemed rather arbitrary to most, but they didn't question the orders that came down from the higher angels. It had been nearly fifteen billion years since the Universe had been created, and angels were now finally allowed to go there under certain strict conditions. One of the stipulations for traveling to the Universe was that they always remain a great distance from Earth—it would take hundreds of millions of years traveling at the ultimate speed to reach it from the training grounds. One of the first lessons drilled into the head of every angel was how their actions influenced the rest of the Universe through the physical laws set down there. The training ground was another planet that was judged a significant distance from anything important that was happening on Earth.

What came to be known as "life" had begun to develop rapidly on Earth following the first cells. The RNA changed its structure slightly and became more stable, losing an "oxy." This new 'de-oxy' RNA or DNA took over the information storage function and RNA was dethroned and subjugated to serving only as a messenger that took the sequence of DNA and arranged small groups of nitrogen-containing acids. It was incredible what these "proteins" could do. They served as structural components, enzymes that brought together multiple chemicals so that they could react with each other, and even special molecules that facilitated the whole process.

That was really the turning point. Alizel had stood at the Portal for millennia on end, just watching the entire process, all the minutest components bonding together and coming into their created purposes. Soon entire cells started collecting together, feeding off each other. One cell swallowed another that was an energy factory and with all that extra energy, it was only a matter of time before it out-replicated the rest.

Cells teamed up with other cells, and the advantage was clear. Soon they started specializing, and a whole host of creatures were born. Animals came out from the sea, great terrible lizards rose and fell, and millions of species were born and either morphed into other species or else died out. Lately, smaller mammals had out replicated the rest to ascend. It was amazing, certainly, but no more so than cleverly arranged sets of atoms. Indeed, it wasn't even really a shock to see them, because they didn't come about all at once. Their complexity arose so gradually over billions of years that there wasn't any single moment that amazed Alizel any more than any other moment.

The evolution of life was made possible by the physical laws of the Universe, but Alizel was amazed at how precisely God had created those laws. There were so many constant values — the attraction of gravity, the mass of the electron, the speed of light in a vacuum, and more. If any one of them was even slightly off, the complexities would never be able to form.

"I never would have thought that these amazing creatures could come from natural laws alone," Alizel confided to Uriel during one of their training sessions. The two of them and their instructor Bodiel were watching the new life forms on Earth from their training planet on the borders of Universe where they couldn't interfere. "Surely God is wonderful," Alizel admitted. "Yet I wonder why it has taken so long? Our world was created in an instant."

"The Lord has other, bigger plans for this world, I think." Uriel winked at Bodiel, who only smiled. At least seven eyes twinkled.

"What could be better than our world?" Alizel wasn't satisfied with the Principality's answer. "God makes His dwelling place with us. He is not going to move to another world, is He?"

"Perhaps the value of that world is in the fact that God is not bodily present," Bodiel said.

"What? How could that make a world better?" Alizel was more confused than before.

"Patience," Bodiel smiled. "I do not pretend to know the Will of God. I have only guesses. But I do know that all will be revealed in time. Things are speeding up. That is all the more reason why we need to get back to your training."

Alizel knew that there was no use arguing with him, and reluctantly prepared for his next lesson.

The lessons were frustrating in themselves. It was so difficult to accomplish even the simplest thing in the Universe. Alizel didn't understand why God had handicapped angels so severely. Although they had been forbidden from interfering with things in the beginning, and still weren't allowed to go to Earth itself, Alizel hoped it was only a matter of time. There was little doubt that they would be called on to shape events on Earth *some* day.

"Now," Bodiel continued, "Uriel, you move that grain of sand to the left, and Alizel, you move it back to the right."

Uriel focused, bringing his hands to his temples. He sent his essence out to the sand, zooming down into the smallest electrons, sending them closer or farther to the nearby atoms, pushing the grain of sand to the left atom by atom. Sweat began to pour down his brow and soak into his chestnut hair. Lines of concentration etched all over his face as the grain slowly moved. As soon as he hit the mark, he dropped his hands and took several deep breaths before wiping his forehead with the back of his hand and fanning himself with his green wings.

"Too hard." Bodiel frowned and shook his head. "You're trying too hard. Our limitations in the Universe are less than they seem. You must use the laws of this world to your advantage."

"How can I make it easier?" Uriel asked. "The same work still needs to be done."

"True," Bodiel replied. "But you need not be the one to do all of it. For example, Alizel, try to move it back."

Alizel braced for the exertion he knew was going to come. He took a deep breath and focused on the grain, ready to jump in.

"But this time, only pull the front edge of the grain."

He brought his fingertips to his temples, pressing inwards to aid in concentration. He found it much easier to move the front edge of the grain, and the back just followed along. It was still difficult, but when he opened his eyes and looked, the grain was back where it began and he was sweating much less than Uriel.

He wiped the sweat away anyway, just to avoid showing up his mentor. Uriel smirked, but seemed pleased with Alizel's success.

"There is more than one way to go about it," Bodiel remarked. "You might try pushing the back edge as well as pulling the front edge. You might try heating the surrounding air to create wind to blow the sand. On Earth, you can use the most powerful method... well, more on that later."

Alizel perked up when he mentioned that forbidden place, but he knew that Bodiel always had a way of making them want to come back for the next lesson. Alizel supposed that's what made him such a good teacher.

"Before we finish..." Bodiel looked directly at a heavy rock on top of a cliff, and wiggled it back and forth with his own essence, finally giving it a push that sent the rock careening over the edge and splashing into the pool of liquid below. "What does that mean?"

Uriel redeemed himself by answering first. "It means all our actions have consequences, intended and unintended, that stretch far into the future. Just as the ripples spread out and lap against distant shores, we must be careful what we set in motion."

Bodiel nodded. "If you learn nothing else, remember this."

Although Alizel still didn't have a clue what his purpose was, at least he wasn't bored anymore. Not only did he have training in the Universe, but he trained at home in Heaven with the new weapons as well. Of course, not everyone wanted to train. But Azazel opened up the weapon hall to anyone who did.

It's amazing how good you can get at something when you have millions of years to practice it, Alizel thought. Since angels weren't hampered by limitations of age or loss of skill and physical agility, their experience only increased while their physical bodies remained strong.

They learned to read their opponents, to feel the vibrations along the edge of the crossed swords and discern their opponents' intentions. They even had enough control that if they did pass through the other's defenses, they could still stop the blade an atom away from their body to avoid hurting them. It was impossible to accidentally strike a friend. They took the time to study the minute shifts in their weight, the barest flutter of an eye that would lead their opponents to telegraph their next technique.

Plus…they could fly.

The angel Zebub spent a good deal of his time at the practice field, and it showed in his skill. He was a Virtue who had hair as white as new snow at dawn and aerodynamic jet black wings. Very few angels had feathers or hair of either color, and Zebub certainly appreciated his appearance. Sometimes when he was conversing with others, he would run his fingers through his hair.

"Welcome, friend!" he called out as Alizel walked down to the practice field. Zebub brought the hilt up to his lips and then swept it downwards. "Care to lose against me again today?"

"It would be an honor to face you." Alizel nodded and swept his open hand from left to right in the form of the salute given when one didn't have a weapon.

"Go sign out a weapon," Zebub said, warming up with a few crisp strikes. "As long as no Powers or Seraphim come by, you can have a shot at me."

Although Alizel knew Zebub was just giving him a good natured ribbing, something about his tone still bothered Alizel. Why was Zebub always so boastful of his abilities? Didn't he know that every skill or strength they had was a gift from God, and nothing more?

Alizel went to see Cantos the attendant and sign out a blade. Though the Seraphim and Azazel all had their own custom made weapons, all of the practice swords were the same.

Alizel took hold of a sword and felt its weight as he rotated it through his fingers. Everything was, of course, perfect. The speed at which he and his fellow angels fought required not one atom to be out of place on the blade.

Satisfied, he saluted Zebub and began.

Zebub sprinted at Alizel with his head and chest parallel to the ground, flapping his wings hard to drive himself forward, but then shaping them downwards to avoid losing contact with the ground, a ground-assault technique they called "assisted running."

Alizel was almost unprepared for this assault, but flung his sword up just in time to block it. Zebub whirled and swung the blade towards Alizel's feet, but he flapped his wings to jump in the air just in time.

Alizel brought his sword downward, but Zebub was there to block it.

Zebub whipped the sword around and held it right in front of Alizel's neck.

His defeat had been quick, but he smiled. "Well done, my friend."

Zebub smiled back as he accepted the praise. "It was, wasn't it? Let's try again. You don't get to my level without a lot of practice!"

Alizel tried again, but the result was the same. Fortunately, he was saved from a third try as Uriel came into view with a sword of his own.

"Hello, Alizel," Uriel said, a twinkle in his large brown eyes. "Would you care to train with me?"

"I would love to, sir," Alizel answered back, grateful for a change in opponents. Zebub smiled and left them to it, as Alizel and Uriel exchanged the salute and began.

They chose an aerial assault, and hovered about a meter above the ground. Uriel swung downwards, and Alizel shifted his weight backwards and laid his body out horizontally, blocking the blow with a loud clang.

Alizel flapped his right wing and spun, and Uriel jumped backwards, crossing his sword downwards to parry Alizel's blow as he barely jumped out of the way. Alizel flapped his white wings again, right and then left immediately afterwards, causing his body to spin in a lethal spiral as it headed towards his Principality.

Uriel's earthy green wings propelled him upwards, his sword arcing downwards as Alizel sped by him and then spun quickly to face him once more.

They could go on like this for hours.

"Very good," Uriel remarked, bringing the hilt up over his heart and sweeping the sword downwards in the traditional salute. "I think that is enough for now."

Alizel returned the salute and they headed back to the armory. They turned in their weapons and Cantos signed them back in.

"Well," he said. "Your improvement over the last hundred years is remarkable."

Alizel thanked him for the compliment.

Alizel and his fellow angels spent a great deal of time in the wonderful gardens that filled Heaven's borders. It wasn't unusual for them to spend years or even decades in quiet contemplation. Rivers of liquid diamond twisted and sparkled as they branched through the soil, nourishing the plant life around them. Each section of the gardens had their own flowers and trees. They had every beautiful flower that had or would ever evolve on Earth, plus so many more that never would. They all blended together to create brilliant combinations, the subtleties of the mixture achieving something that was more than the sum of its parts.

Alizel came across Eleleth and Abbadon sitting together on a bench talking quietly during one such excursion. Those two had always been close to each other, almost like they were two sides to the same coin.

Marriage was not a concept angels were familiar with, at least not in the way that humans would come to think of it many years later. The bond felt in marriage was really a sharing of the love and power of God between two souls. Alizel felt that close to each and every angel in Heaven, because that was the way they were connected.

Angels also had neither need nor desire to reproduce. The whole idea of reproduction was strange to them. They saw the vital role it played on Earth amongst the new creatures living there, but every angel alive had existed from the beginning. No one was older or younger than another. On Earth, the makeup of a population changed as some organisms reproduced more than others. As the environment changed, so too did the creatures who were suited for it. Yet, angels were already perfect. They had no need to evolve into anything else.

If angels did have marriage, though, Eleleth and Abbadon would certainly have been the ideal couple. Alizel rarely saw them apart.

Alizel waited out of earshot, but gradually meandered over into their field of view and stopped when he was sure that they had seen him, the polite way of waiting for them to finish their conversation and not interrupting. He waited a while. It might have been an hour, a day, or a week. He wasn't really sure, and time had even less meaning inside of the gardens of Heaven. Alizel felt perfectly comfortable just sitting and contemplating a flower for a year or more. Even though he could move at the speed of light and completely understand a thing instantaneously, sometimes it was worth it to just sit and think deeply about the wonder of God.

"Come on over, Alizel!" Abbadon waved to him. He usually spoke first when he was with Eleleth. Abbadon had always been a large angel, strong and toned. He had a commanding presence in his black robes, yet he didn't seem dangerous in the way that the Power Azazel did. Yet perhaps that was just because of the influence of the one sitting beside him.

Eleleth smiled and nodded her invitation, and Alizel covered the distance to where they were sitting in a few strides. Eleleth was wearing a simple white alb that flowed as easily around the curves of her body as her golden hair flowed across the contours of her shoulders. As always, her robe was perfectly spotless.

"We were just marveling at the beauty and serenity here," she remarked, looking around as if seeing everything for the first time. It was one of the most remarkable facets of the Garden. If an angel looked away and then looked back, the wonder he had just seen would be gone, with a new and equally splendid one in its place.

"Do you think it's true?" Abbadon looked directly at Alizel. "Could someone ever come to destroy this place?"

It was quite a direct question, but Abbadon was never one to fear action or directness. Alizel shrugged his shoulders. "I can't imagine it, but I also admit that I never foresaw the evolution of life in the Universe either, so I may not be the one to say one way or another."

Eleleth looked around again. "Surely we must also consider the benevolence of the Lord. He wishes us to live in peace because that is how He created us. Why then would He create others who could do us harm? Why would He create a wonder such as this garden only to let it be destroyed?"

"You're probably right," Abbadon agreed, and smoothed a hand through his blood-red hair thoughtfully. "Besides, God did create Azazel and the Powers to protect Heaven and hold the border between the Realm of Spirit and the Realm of Matter. Certainly they would be strong enough to defeat anything that could come through the Portal."

"I do not even see how any creature from the Universe could ever be strong enough to come here," Eleleth mused. "After all, we can enter freely into the Universe and thus our spirits can exist there. Yet, there is no matter here in Heaven. The creatures in the Realm of Matter are made only of matter, without a spiritual component. So it seems as if things can go only one way. Those from Heaven can go to the Universe. Spirit can go to matter, but not the other way around. Could a material creature even exist in a spiritual world?"

Alizel had never thought of that. "You're right…they would need to have a spiritual part, and also be able to separate it from their physical part. I do not see how such a thing could ever evolve. But it's all speculation when we're dealing with the wonder of God's creation."

They spoke on like this for a long time, finally going their own ways to contemplate the beauty that was in the gardens, secure that none could ever come from the Universe to destroy them.

CHAPTER THREE:

ZEBUB'S REBELLION

Time went by, and the complexity of life on Earth increased exponentially. Some of the mammals could even work in groups or use tools. Alizel found new wonders to observe and contemplate nearly every time he visited the Portal, or whenever Bodiel took him and the others to their training ground in the Universe. Earth was beginning to teem with activity.

It was about this time that the trouble in Heaven really started.

Ever since life had begun to develop, there had been questionings of God's plan. Most, like Alizel, had been content to wait and see what He developed. Angels had never been in need before, never been led astray by God. But perhaps that was the problem.

Alizel never expected anything to come of the grumblings. And he never thought that his friends would have been capable of such an act.

He couldn't say that it started out of boredom, but even angels can get restless after fifteen billion years.

He was at the training grounds one day while Verin and Zebub were in a particularly contentious match.

"I told you you're no match for me," Zebub was saying as he parried blow after blow from Verin. "You are so hasty. There's no subtlety in your attack. Take your time and don't telegraph your movements!"

"You're not the only one who knows what he's doing!" Instead of heeding Zebub's words, Verin did the opposite and doubled down on his previous strategy. "I'm too fast for you!"

Alizel cringed watching Verin's dogged determination. What was the rush? If he would just slow down and think things through, he would make much better decisions. As it was, he had no hope of beating Zebub.

Zebub was playing with him now, slicing off tufts of Verin's fire-red hair and laughing.

Alizel became uneasy. Something about how Zebub was doing it made Alizel feel things he hadn't felt before. Something was very wrong, almost as if Zebub was enjoying Verin's distress.

Cantos must have felt it too, for he came over and halted them in their duel. They immediately broke apart.

Verin stood there, fuming.

Alizel frowned, watching his friend. Did he notice something dark behind those eyes? Alizel was relieved to see that Cantos had a Principality and a Power standing behind him.

"I think that is enough for now," Cantos intoned, his voice stone serious. He held out his hand. "It is time to turn your weapons back in."

Zebub started to hand his sword over, although his face showed that he very much disliked being told what to do by someone who didn't share his skills with the blade.

"You too," Cantos said to Verin, who looked like handing over his sword was the last thing he wanted to do. When he didn't move, Cantos reached out gently to grab the pommel.

Verin held it fast, so Cantos tugged a little harder.

In a flash, Verin swung the sword straight at him. The desk keeper's face showed the slightest hint of shock before the blade hit him.

An angel's sword didn't cut, but as it touched his body, Cantos screamed. Angels had no conception of pain, so Alizel wasn't sure what it was. But he soon saw its effects. Instantly, Cantos's whole body shimmered and shivered, iridescent hues running from the tip of his toes to the ends of his feathers. And then, just as suddenly as it had started, he was gone.

There was a moment where the world hung frozen. The enormity of what had just happened washed over all of them. For the first time, ever, something had changed in a way that it would never go back.

The word "broken" entered the angels' collective knowledge.

In the instant they recovered, Verin struck again, panicked. He hit the defenseless Principality, who screamed and disappeared just as Cantos had done.

"Verin!" Alizel wanted to stop him, wanted to keep things from spiraling out of control, but he didn't know what to do. Zebub and Verin were the only ones who had swords!

Verin turned to face the Power, but Zebub had already taken care of him.

He looked to Alizel, and Alizel was frightened by what he saw in the other's eyes. Verin was scared too, only understanding a shade of what had transpired.

Zebub kept a level head. He grabbed Verin by the shoulder to gain his attention again, and Alizel saw their determination to protect each other in the chaos that was sure to ensue.

Without even thinking, Verin and Zebub launched into the air with two flaps of their great wings, and were gone.

Alizel felt something running down his cheek. He reached his hand up and realized that it was a tear. What a strange thing… He had cried before, many times. Yet those had always been tears of joy at the wonder of God. He did not know that tears could also come out in sorrow. The immediate danger past, Alizel buried his face in his hands, sank to his knees and wept bitterly.

Rather than chasing immediately, the other angels mourned. They cried, for what they had feared had come true. None wept harder than Eleleth.

Despite the fact that God could open up the Containment if He wanted to, Alizel knew deep within him that all of this, this feeling inside his heart, this sorrow in Heaven, was something fundamentally new. Things were going so terribly wrong.

He thought that would be the end of it when Azazel went after the two refugees, but for some reason he could not find them. He had all his resources dedicated to securing the borders of Heaven; he was not prepared for an attack from within.

Yet an odd thing happened.

They became a magnet.

Everyone who was dissatisfied with the rules of Heaven, or who thought that God had neglected them, or taken advantage of them, or was just fed up with living in Heaven as it was set off after them to join them. Alizel had thought that his fellow angels were satisfied. After all, how could they be unhappy when they lived a perfect immortal life? What could cause someone to throw that away? With Verin and Zebub, it had been a combination of pride and impatience. Alizel was sure that they would regret it. He couldn't understand why they did not just come back to God and beg for forgiveness. Would God really turn away from His own creation?

Perhaps if it had just been the two of them, maybe they would have come back. Alizel certainly held out hope. But when other angels joined them, Alizel knew it was too much for Zebub. He would love to be in command.

Alizel knew of a few angels who joined them. Kasadya, a Principality who rarely showed any emotion, was among the first. Alizel was grieved to learn that Abbadon followed him shortly afterward, though it didn't fully surprise him. It seemed that Abbadon just wanted to be in the middle of everything that was happening. Eleleth's beautiful face seemed to darken and her large eyes often were shiny with tears after that.

Alizel wanted nothing more than to ignore the rebellion and just go about his normal routine, pretending everything would go back to the way it used to be…but it was impossible. Nothing like this had ever happened before, and it was all anyone wanted to talk about.

Even if he had been able to concentrate, his normal routine was off limits. He couldn't go down to the Universe anymore; Azazel had sealed off the borders of Heaven to prevent any of the rebels from escaping. And there was no way that anyone was going to open the armory for weapons practice.

It was a few weeks after the rebellion started that Alizel was meditating in one of the common rooms when he heard an urgent whisper.

"Alizel!" The voice was all too familiar, although it now held a strange harshness to it. Alizel was relieved to hear him, but at the same time wished he would go away.

"Verin," he turned to face his friend, "what are you doing here? What if someone sees you?"

"It's a risk I had to take," he replied, pausing to glance around the room and make sure no one was listening. "You need to know what is happening."

Alizel raised his eyebrows, intrigued but confused. "Tell me."

Verin's eyes darted back and forth, intently scanning the walls as if he could see through them and see hunters on the other side. His face was ragged, his bearing unsure and scared. He did not have the sword that he had stolen.

"They're completely messing everything up. What do we have now? 'Toy' worlds that take forever and serve as nothing but amusement, weapons that we practice with for millennia but can't use, and a leader who really doesn't care what happens to us!"

"Things might not seem perfect," Alizel was defensive, "but we must trust in God. He has not led us astray."

"How long, Alizel?" Verin asked, shaking his head. "How long must we wait? Fifteen billion Earth years? I say that's enough! God's had His chance to run things. Now it's time for someone more competent to step in and take over."

Alizel stepped back, shocked. This was bordering on blasphemy. "More competent? God made this entire world! None of us could ever have done that. We didn't even exist to be able to do something like that."

Surely, something had driven Verin crazy.

"Okay," he said, putting up his hands as if to ward off Alizel's incredulity. "So God does know how to make a world, we're grateful to Him for that. But just because He created the world doesn't mean He knows what to do with it. I think it's pretty obvious that He doesn't."

"Not everyone agrees that things are as bad as you think they are," Alizel growled. Uriel's gentle tutelage came to mind. "I, for one, think our leaders are doing an excellent job."

"An excellent job of what? Sitting back and doing nothing? Excuse me if I'm not overly impressed. Even I could do well leading a bunch of angels with no ambition to the Wonderful Land of Nowhere."

"But why now? If we've waited this long, surely we could wait a little longer. Things are starting to happen on Earth. Look at the creatures that have evolved there!"

"Like it or not," Verin countered, "things have started to happen here too. We can't go back to how things were before we ended those angels' existences."

Alizel's heart sank: Verin's voice carried not even the barest hint of regret.

"I need to ask you something." Verin lowered his voice and stared Alizel in the eye. "You have always been one of my closest friends...can I count on you to stand with us again?"

Alizel was aghast, and angry. His friend *was* crazy. "Go against God? And just how do you plan on winning? Will you end His existence too? Will you stand against Him with the weapon He forged?"

Verin smiled for the first time, a slow, unnerving grin that reached only halfway across his face. "We won't need to. We'll simply end enough angels' existences that He is forced to let Zebub take over as the Ruler of Heaven."

The reality of Verin's insanity and outright rejection of the Father's rule paralyzed Alizel. He could only stare back at him in shock, and anger, only then realizing just how far Verin had slid. To destroy enough of Heaven that God would fear? This was madness! His only consolation was that the plan was doomed to failure by the sheer lunacy of it.

Since Alizel didn't answer for a few moments, Verin repeated his point. "We'll send enough of them into the Containment that He'll have no other choice!"

"Well then," a voice materialized from the doorway, "why don't you start with me?"

They both whirled to see Azazel standing in the door, sword calmly held at his side.

"Don't just stand there with your jaw dropped to the floor," he continued, looking not the least bit worried. "You want to end some angel's existence? Here I am."

He kept the point of his sword lowered, daring Verin to strike first. Alizel wanted to throw himself in between them and protect his friend, but he was frozen both from Verin's unthinkable utterances and Azazel's commanding presence.

Nothing about Verin's bearing gave the least indication that he had any intention of fighting Azazel, but he did look like he was about to throw a taunt in his face. His lips twisted with the effort of keeping it back, and then he turned and bolted as he thought better of it. Verin had no chance. The fight would have probably have been about even if Verin had a sword and Azazel was unarmed, but the reverse was true.

Azazel was after him, a golden streak racing into the corridors, sword held out in front of him. Verin had dashed through the opening in the wall, going this way and that through rooms and corridors, startling angels and trying to throw them into Azazel's path.

Verin was lucky, and he was fast. He knew where he was going, and as Alizel flew upwards above the buildings to try to see the chase, he could tell that Verin was going to escape. He was crossing back on his original path, causing Azazel to have to backtrack and switch directions over and over. Alizel didn't want the Power to touch his friend with the sword, but he couldn't say he was entirely happy that he escaped either.

He knew Azazel should have been frustrated when he returned, but he couldn't tell if he was or not. Azazel never seemed to show any emotion on the outside.

Verin's conversation stayed in Alizel's mind for the next few days. He couldn't believe what he was suggesting. What had happened to cause his friend to become so crazy? He wanted to end the existence of as many angels as possible!

Fortunately, the rebellion was hampered by the fact that they only had the two original swords that Verin and Zebub had stolen.

It was shortly after that time when something remarkable and even more disconcerting happened. No one really knew how important it was at the time, although they all had hints. The first time Alizel noticed anything amiss was one day when he was walking by the Portal. Mupiel was there, his excited eyes shining, and he waved Alizel over.

He saw the glint of the Realm of Matter below. The Portal was open. What could this mean? Had the rebellion finally been crushed? What had happened to Verin? He saw Azazel himself standing at attention near the Portal's entrance.

"Does this mean that the trouble is over, sir?" Alizel felt excitement rush throughout his body. "Can we go down to the Universe again?"

"No," he answered crisply. "We've just opened it for a brief moment for someone to pass through." Azazel didn't seem too happy about it as his silver eyes scanned the horizon, almost daring one of the rebels to come and try to sneak away.

If Azazel didn't want the Portal opened, that meant that someone had overruled him. But as chief angel in charge of the defense of Heaven, who could have done so?

Alizel glanced at Mupiel, who shrugged. Azazel didn't look like he wanted to answer any more questions, but Alizel's curiosity was too strong. "Excuse me, sir. But might I ask who is going to be passing through?"

He stood there, immobile. Alizel wasn't sure if he had heard his question or not, but suddenly Uriel was beside him.

"See for yourself," he said, pointing.

Alizel turned, and saw not one angel, but several. They weren't the common angels either, but Cherubim, twelve in front. The Cherubim had four wings instead of two, two large ones coming out of the back, plus two smaller ones underneath. The smaller set often wrapped around the front, obscuring their white sash and golden "C". There was no mistaking any angel of this order. They had been created with four faces too. Alizel wasn't sure why, but the rumor was that they had been given this blessing so that wherever they were, whatever they did, they never had to turn away from God. Even when their back was to Him, they were still looking straight at Him.

Suddenly, Alizel knew who was going to go through the Portal. There was only one being who commanded a full honor guard.

It was the Father.

God Himself was going down to the Universe.

What could He be doing down there? Alizel wanted to rush into the Portal and follow Him, but he knew Azazel would never allow it.

God was everything at once, glory burning so brightly and intensely that Alizel couldn't even focus his gaze on Him, let alone describe Him. Raging fire, blinding light…none of those even came close to capturing the essence of who He was. He was really a They, different personas blending and separate all the same.

His essence passed through, and the Portal closed itself behind Him, and Alizel sighed, resigned to the thought that whatever God did down there would be closed off to angels for all eternity.

Or…so he thought.

"*Watch.*"

Alizel felt a shiver run through him as God suddenly spoke. The insides of Heaven opened up, allowing the angels to see everything happening, even though they couldn't go down to the Universe itself.

Everywhere at once, God didn't travel to Earth. He simply filled the Universe and was there. The angels watched as he made His presence known in the fertile lands of the Earth, all of the creation moving under His essence.

He moved next to some of the more intelligent mammals, gathering troops of them together. They moved towards their Creator, obedient but unknowing. Alizel still marveled at the creatures that had evolved by the natural laws God had set down in the world. They had even developed primitive intelligence, the ability to solve problems and work as a unit. But they were still nothing more than neurons responding in deterministic fashion, given their inputs of accumulated experience. A bird that flew in the wind was no different than a leaf that blew in the same wind. A primate that made a tool was no different than a beaver that made a dam. If any of the animals were conscious, it was but an illusion.

All that was about to change in a big way.

"*Come,*" God said to one of them, "*Come and have life.*"

He breathed on the animal, and something changed in his eyes. His movement became more purposeful, his intelligence greater, his body just a shade heavier. Alizel didn't know what was different, but he saw him in a different light. It almost looked like there was an angel inside of him, interacting with him by pushing electrons through the brain, causing thoughts.

"*You shall be Adam.*" God said, as the new creature looked on in wonder. Alizel thought him new because although he still looked like the others, there was something fundamentally different about him. God turned to Adam's mate and said "*And you shall be Eve.*"

It seemed like such a simple thing, really. But that's the way things were with God. He could do grandiose things like creating an entire intricate natural world, and His tone of voice was calm and relaxed. He was never in the least bit pretentious. After all, who would He have to impress?

He continued on, breathing on several more of the mammals and giving them each the new intangible essence. Yet, as Alizel watched Him the amazing thing was that each one was a little different than the rest. There were similarities to be sure, but each essence was distinct, just as each angel was different from the others.

So God had created the humans in two steps. First He had created a world where soulless creatures could evolve, and then He had taken the extraordinary step of fusing a component from the Realm of Spirit to their bodies. Alizel remembered his conversation with Eleleth and Abbadon in the garden. Could the souls now enter Heaven? Why had God done it this way?

"*I have given you life.*" As He spoke, they all looked in wonder at themselves, as if seeing their arms and legs for the very first time.

"Who are you?" the one called Adam asked. "Who are we?"

"*I am the Lord, your God,*" He answered. "*And you are My people. I have formed you, and give you dominion over this world that I have created.*"

Adam looked around in wonder, as if seeing everything around them for the very first time. He looked at Eve, and a big smile came across his face.

"What are we to do here?" she asked.

"*I have given you everything that you need,*" God answered. "*The trees produce fruit for you. The animals produce meat for you. The rivers give you abundant water to quench your thirst, and the fields will bring forth grain when properly tilled. You shall have everything you need to live here. And I shall love you.*"

God came back through the Portal and Azazel closed it after Him. Though He was present everywhere both in the Universe and in Heaven, God had never entirely revealed Himself on Earth in this way before.

"What could this mean?" Alizel asked Uriel. From his furrowed brow and downcast eyes, it was obvious the Principality didn't have any more information than he did.

"It's almost like He made them like us," Uriel mused.

"But they're not," Alizel replied, dumb-founded. "Look at them— they're made out of atoms. They aren't made out of the same stuff as us."

Mupiel pursed his lips, thoughtfully. "I wonder if they can cross to Heaven? I mean, if Azazel opened the barrier."

"Perhaps that's why God forged the weapons for Azazel…" Uriel nodded slowly as if things were falling into place. After the three angels had been sent into the Containment, there had been much debate in Heaven. Had God made a mistake in allowing the weapons to be made? The idea of God doing something wrong was so foreign that most of the angels dismissed it out of hand. However, as the rebellion continued, thoughts turned to words, and words turned to heated debate. What if God had led them astray on this issue? If He was fallible, where else might He fail to protect them?

"I see…" Alizel smiled, following the Principality's train of thought. "So maybe making the weapons was part of his plan all along. He knew that they would cause a small problem in Heaven, but they would protect us against an even greater threat."

"I don't know," Mupiel spoke up. "Why wouldn't God just make the barrier stronger, then? Or make those new creatures weaker?" The idea of a tradeoff was new to the angels. They had never seen God do anything that would lead them to believe that He didn't have absolute power and control over every situation.

Alizel was about to reply when he felt the call for a meeting in the Angelarch. It wrapped over his body, pulling him onward. He welcomed the intrusion. He looked to his companions and saw that they felt it too.

"Let's hope they have some answers…"

The stadium was more packed than Alizel had ever seen it. But this was an unprecedented event. Things were starting to happen so fast… Just centuries ago everything had been just as it always was. Angels were foolish to wish for change, he realized. Change for its own sake was no good when the life you had was already perfect.

As far as Alizel remembered, which was pretty much since the creation of Heaven, God had never left His throne. Now, not only had He left it, but He had gone down into the Universe and done something the angels didn't understand. At least, Alizel didn't. Maybe some of the superiors could shed some light on the whole affair.

The Angelarch was alive with an electrified murmur of conversation. The high stadium walls shone with the reflected light of God's Energy, silken banners of each of the nine orders of angels flapping in the zephyr that came down from Mt. Zion. Each order's banner matched the color and letter of its sash.

Alizel glanced around at the hubbub, and suddenly missed Verin and Abbadon's presence in the seats above him. He hoped desperately that they would be able to return soon.

Berachiel, the head of the Dominions, seemed to be the most excited, Alizel noticed, the angel's green eyes sparkling as if he had just suddenly found his purpose. Yet most angels were more nervous or shocked than excited.

Silence shot through the crowd as Luciferel rose to speak. If anyone would know what was going on, it would probably be him or one of the Cherubim. He seemed unperturbed, his smile naturally flowing across his face and his platinum hair neat and in place. His blood red wings unfolded gracefully as he rose. Alizel wasn't sure if his serenity was a good omen or not. If he knew and wasn't worried, that was a good sign. However, even if he didn't know, Alizel couldn't see anything shaking the Seraph's trust in God.

"Today is a momentous day," he began with a huge understatement. "For the Lord God has seen fit to fundamentally change one species of the creatures on Earth. He has chosen to give them part of Himself, an essence unique to each individual creature. This He has called a 'soul' and the new race of creatures He has created is the Race of Man. They are to be called 'humans' and will have dominion over the Earth just as angels have dominion over Heaven."

"Are they really so like us?" Raphael asked. Alizel thought he sounded perturbed. "Is this Earth to be another Heaven?"

"Certainly not," Luciferel replied. "They are like us in that each is an autonomous individual, free to make his or her own decisions. But there are many important differences. We are made of the glory of God— Sons of Fire. They are made of the Earth— Sons of Clay. While we have always existed, these humans live and die according to the natural laws of the Universe, just as other creatures do.

"The creatures die," Luciferel continued, "but the souls cannot. How can something that is a part of God perish? The Lord has not said what will happen to those souls once their hosts can no longer sustain them. I do not pretend to know what He intends."

Alizel sighed. At least the angels now knew what had happened. Although, as always, it seemed the why of it was just beyond their reach.

"What is the purpose of this dual system?" Eleleth mused. "How will our world and their world interact with each other?"

"We should not assume that there are only two worlds," Raphael interjected, looking off toward the Portal. "Perhaps this Earth is only the first. Perhaps the Lord will create many Universes, or place human life in other places in this Universe."

"He may yet," answered Gabriel, his ash-blond curls bouncing as he turned his head toward his fellow Seraph. "But I do not think this is likely. I believe that two worlds are all He needs to serve His purpose."

Alizel tried to drink in the words of the wiser angels. They were giving so many answers and explanations all of a sudden. It didn't matter that they were little more than supposition, or that God frequently sprung surprises on them. At least the Seraphim were saying what they thought, rather than just keeping it to themselves.

The whole assembly was in rapt attention. It seemed like just about everyone was there...but something felt off to Alizel. His eyes roamed the crowd, looking for any clue as to why he felt uneasy. He saw Semyaza, an unranked with a square jaw and hard eyes, though Alizel noticed his eyes had softened somewhat now, probably astounded at the beauty God had created on Earth. Alizel also noticed the Dominion Gagiel, awestruck as everyone else. Alizel glanced up at the Powers section, which was surprisingly almost full. That disturbed him somewhat, because that meant...

The scream echoed through Heaven. Every single angel felt it in their core, a part of the communal bond destroyed.

A life had been snuffed out, then another, and another.

The rebels had struck while the others were all occupied, and taken the one place the angels had so foolishly left vulnerable. The one place they needed more than anything.

They had taken the armory.

"Angels, hear me now!" Zebub bellowed, sweeping into the arena, a sword held lustily in each hand. He spread his sleek black wings out to their full span. "How much more foolishness will it take? What more do you need to see before you join us?"

Alizel jumped up. It seemed everyone was scrambling around at once. The revolution had always been something intangible, something that lurked in the shadows and never came out to openly challenge God's authority. For the first time, they showed themselves at their full strength.

There were nearly fifty of them, barely noticeable against the thousands and thousands of loyalists, but their advantage was clear. They all had swords now.

Alizel scanned their faces, and finally found Verin's. Abbadon was beside him, and it pained Alizel to see his friends so happily among the rebels. How could they not doubt their plan to usurp God's rule? How could they accept the destruction of another soul?

Luciferel's commanding voice rose above the chaos. "What do you need to see before you give up your foolish ways and return to God?" he challenged. "You cannot defeat us. You cannot go against the power of the Most High!"

"We cannot?" Verin flew to hover beside his new master, eyes aglow. "Who is anyone here to tell us what we cannot do, when we are the ones holding the swords? We cannot kill you? Watch us."

"Then let me be the first." Azazel's calm voice seemed out of place with the blinding flash as his sword leapt into his hand. A few of the Seraphim and Powers always wore their weapons. At least they were not totally unprepared.

He raised his eyebrows. "Well? I'm waiting."

Verin and Zebub took a step forward, their eyes aflame.

"Stop!" Eleleth threw her body between the two sides, only a few meters apart now. There were tears in her eyes. "Surely it has not come to this? Put away your swords, I beg of you."

Eleleth was one of the most beloved angels, always kind and gentle. Alizel suddenly realized, clutching the railing where he stood, that she was perhaps their last hope. If anyone could soften hard hearts, it would be her.

Eleleth searched for her soul mate's face, and found him in the crowd of rebels behind Verin and Zebub.

"Abbadon, please. Think of the days we used to walk in the gardens. Think of the sweet flowers we used to smell, the peace that we have lived with. Would you throw that all away?"

His answer was automatic, almost as if he didn't trust himself to think about it. "We have put up with peace for too long." His silver wings snapped out in anger. "It is time for a different way."

Eleleth was visibly shaken by Abbadon's candor. "Azazel," she turned to the Power. "This is not your task. Please, let us put away your weapons." It was clear that Eleleth couldn't bear a grudge after the way that she had forgiven Azazel for asking to make the swords in the first place. The hints came through sometimes, though, in the way she always referred to all the swords as somehow belonging to him.

"My task has always been to defend Heaven— from all enemies inside and out." His answer was more automatic than Abbadon's.

Eleleth cast her eyes about frantically, trying to appeal to anyone, searching for the faintest crack in the wall that they had thrust up between them. Zebub was obviously not going to listen. She settled on Verin as their last hope. Though intimidating in his own right, of everyone standing there, Verin was probably the weakest.

"Verin, please, convince Zebub. Do not be hasty," she pleaded, pain on her face. "Let us find another way."

His face softened for a minute even as Alizel's brightened. Perhaps this slaughter could be avoided…

His face lost the look of compassion as quickly as it had sprung up. "We've wasted enough time already." His sword rang as he drew it from its sheath.

Abbadon's did the same even as he cried out, "All who stand in our way shall be destroyed!"

They swung for Eleleth.

Luciferel barely had time to dive for her before the blades rent the empty air. With a fierce cry, the fifty lost angels started attacking.

Even for someone who can journey through the entire Universe with the swiftness of thought, everything started happening at once. The angelic forms were more than a hundred thousand blurs.

"Powers, fly to me! Others stand behind!" Azazel's words broke through the din, and Alizel saw several Powers and Seraphim fly off to make the shell of half a sphere. Immediately Alizel understood. They would take the brunt of the assault, and protect the others. If the traitors tried to fly around, they could just rotate the direction the hemisphere was facing.

Zebub's minions hacked away right and left at those who were defenseless, their blades striking angels and sending them to the void. Some were caught up and overwhelmed by sheer numbers of brave loyalists, and once their swords were wrestled from their grasps they were either destroyed or bound.

On the front lines the battle was fierce. Zebub's advantage lessened more and more as the loyalists managed to wrest swords away from his fighters. The most trained and powerful angels now stood before him in the half-sphere, and Zebub was at a big numerical disadvantage.

Zebub concentrated his forces on the center point of the sphere, trying to break through the protective shield. He sent two angels streaking in front of him with swords held forwards, a risky but powerful move. They would try to force an enemy to move out of the way, but if he was swift enough to dodge and counter, the attacker would be caught in a position where he could not easily block the counterattack. The slightest touch from a Heaven's Blade on any part of the body was enough to send an angel to the Containment. Considering the number and power of the angels holding the front of the half-sphere, it was suicide.

Luciferel, Michael, and Azazel hovered there, dispatching enemies right and left. They often trained together, and were making use of their combined powers. Even solo, they were the three angels most skilled with the blade in all of Heaven. Combined, no one was a match for them. Michael and Azazel met Zebub's two guards streaking toward them, and dove to the sides just in time, whipping back and striking them with their blades.

Zebub drew himself up as he saw his two front guards perish. He looked at the stern-faced angels barring his way, and appeared to be thinking twice about attacking. The silver jewel in the pommel of Luciferel's sword burned brightly with a holy fury that didn't cast any shadows on his crimson blade. Raphael drew himself up next to Azazel, as if the head of the Powers needed any more help. Michael's eyes were ablaze.

Zebub hadn't staved off destruction for this long by being foolish. Fear hit his eyes as he turned to fly away, sending two more guards at the trio. The rest of his forces he ordered into a hasty retreat.

"I'll handle these," Azazel said hungrily, a gold and platinum streak that headed for the guards.

"We'll catch the rest," Michael finished, racing off after Zebub. Luciferel followed close behind.

Alizel stared steadily at the gentle Raphael, and saw the tears that gleamed in his eyes.

They did catch them, or at least most of them. Alizel learned that much the following week after the hunt had died down. He was walking through one of the heavenly forests one day, and spotted Gabriel and Luciferel nearby. At the time Alizel didn't know how important their conversation would be to the future of Heaven—and Earth. When Luciferel began with the words "You may tell the others," Alizel felt justified in perking his ears up to listen.

"You may tell the others," Luciferel said, frowning slightly, "that the revolution is all but broken." Though the news was good, he seemed to blame himself that it wasn't perfect. "Zebub," he spat the name as if bile was in his mouth, "has still eluded us, though most of his companions have been caught or destroyed."

Gabriel nodded. As chief messenger, it was his responsibility to manage the flow of information in Heaven. "Excellent work, Bright One of God. It seems only a matter of time, then. After his brashness in attacking the Angelarch, he isn't likely to get support from anyone."

"It was foolish," Luciferel agreed. "But no more foolish than opposing God in the first place. And their plan of destroying angels until God relinquishes His control over Heaven...it's laughable. It would never work."

"I do not think that there is any plan that could cause God to give up Heaven," Gabriel chuckled.

It was good to see Gabriel laugh. There hadn't been enough of that in Heaven lately.

"There is one plan..." Luciferel said it softly, almost to himself. "One that I am certain would work."

Gabriel raised his eyebrows to encourage him to go on. Alizel, from his hiding spot, unconsciously did the same.

Now it was Luciferel's turn to laugh. "I think it would be wise to keep this in the silence of my own heart. You never know where eavesdroppers may be lurking."

Sweat started dripping down Alizel's brow. Could they see him? What would they do if he was caught? Alizel had seen the way that Luciferel mowed down the traitors. Just as Alizel was thinking of how he could explain that he wasn't part of the resistance, Gabriel changed the subject and they continued talking.

"God never ceases to amaze me. To think that He made those creatures, those...humans, using only the natural laws of the Universe, and their intelligence evolved to the point where he could give them souls." He shook his head in wonder.

"The Lord is incredible," Luciferel agreed. "But I must admit that the humans do not impress me. Their only value more than a rock or tree or animal comes from the piece of the Almighty inside of them."

"Not a thing to be taken lightly," Gabriel reminded, folding his snow grey wings closer to his body.

"Certainly not. But look at them." Luciferel's voice took on a hint of disdain. "Their perceptions are constrained by what their senses can tell them. Take their eyes, for instance. They can see only a fraction of the electromagnetic spectrum. And even with what they can see, they can only look for a distance, and only see things on the same scale as themselves. They can no sooner look and see a distant galaxy than they can see the inside of an atom."

"Maybe their value lies in their limitations."

"You say it like I haven't heard those rumors." Luciferel's mood was turning darker now. Alizel had never seen him like this before. What were the rumors? Why did they bother him so?

Gabriel held up his hands to distance himself from the conversation that was rapidly turning into an argument. "I'm just saying, what if what we value isn't always what God values?"

"It's not a matter of value! It's a matter of spending billions of years on a Universe just to produce limited beings."

"Maybe they have something that we don't. Something we can't comprehend."

"I don't believe that," Luciferel retorted. His red wings flared. "What could they possibly have that we lack? You can see them too. We're so much more than they are. They can barely even live for more than a hundred years."

"They may live for longer with the divine spark inside of them," Gabriel suggested. "We can't really know how that will affect them."

"There's no doubt that it will affect them for the better. But anyone who thinks that that will put them on the same level as us is a sheer lunatic. A small breath from God is nothing to underestimate, but our entire beings are fueled by direct energy from the Father. There's no comparison."

Gabriel nodded, more for acknowledgement than agreement. "In any event, we must set our sights on cleaning up the last remaining shreds of this resistance and trust to God that He will reveal the place of these humans in His master plan."

"That's the most sensible thing you've said in a while," Luciferel smiled naturally as he spoke. He hungrily fingered the serpentine hilt of his sword. The blade of Lucifer's sword was the elongated tongue of a dragon, while the body coiled around his hand and wrist to protect it. He nodded goodbye to Gabriel and took flight. Alizel watched him go until he was out of sight and then slowly crept away.

For some reason, that conversation stayed with Alizel. Any creature of matter had a brain that was finite— limited by the number of neurons and the connections between them. Angels didn't exist in the physical world as such, and thus did not share those limitations. Everything that had ever happened— everything—was stored so that they could access it at any time simply by thinking about it. If humans had had that capability, they would have been able to remember every sunset ever seen or book ever read. There was no need to make records and fewer arguments occurred, as every angel always remembered exactly what had happened at every moment since Heaven had been formed, so long as he had witnessed it firsthand.

So while he could instantly access any of the conversations that he had ever had, this one kept playing in Alizel's mind. He went through it over and over, trying to find out anything that he had missed. Alizel tried to read between the lines, to see if the two Seraphim had meant more than what they had said. Luciferel was their leader, of course, but as chief messenger, Gabriel might know something no one else did. Alizel tried to ask a Cherub named

Hanael about God's plan for the humans once, but the conversation was pretty much a failure.

"Excuse me, sir..." Alizel tapped him on one shoulder. "May I ask you a question?"

The Cherub stood there as if he hadn't heard him, his body facing toward the Throne of God. His eyes were focused straight ahead.

"Sir, this will only take a minute of your time. I was just wondering..."

Still nothing. Alizel tried waving his hand in front of the Cherub's face closest to him. He wasn't trying to be disrespectful, but Hanael could at least acknowledge him. This was enough to cause him to notice Alizel. Two of his other faces frowned in annoyance, while the third still faced God.

The eyes of the closest face focused on him.

"I'm sorry, did you say something?"

"Yes sir. It's just that...I'm confused with all these new things happening on Earth and with God's plan, and I...I just don't know quite what to make of it. You see..."

But at that very moment Hanael dashed off. "I'm sorry, I have to go now," he mumbled absentmindedly. He might have said something like "important business" or "what nonsense is this?" It didn't really matter.

Cherubim weren't the greatest communicators.

CHAPTER FOUR:

GOD'S PLAN REVEALED

The angels had waited billions of years until the humans gained souls, and even though things were accelerating, there was no reason to think that they wouldn't wait billions more to find out why.

So it was certainly shocking when the Father Himself simply announced His purpose mere days later.

"It is I."

Alizel started when he felt the words and looked in the direction of the Throne of God, and saw everyone around him do the same. "Felt" was even the wrong word for it. It was just something that he knew. They had never been communicated to in this way before, except for at the very Beginning. God was talking to His angels directly.

"My plans on Earth are now being set in motion. The humans are very special creatures to Me. They will be My people."

Alizel's brows furrowed. The *humans* were His people now?

"You, My beloved angels, will act to serve and guide them."

The Father's words felt like a stone dropped into a tranquil lake, the shock of what He said rippling through Heaven. Serve them? Was there some mistake? Yet, there could be no mistaking the Father's words or meaning. There was no misunderstanding when talking with God.

"You will always be close to my heart. But the Humans must serve a different purpose. Your service is freely given, but you have known Me

intimately. What reward is in that? Will the Humans, who cannot see Me and do not know Me the way that you do, choose Me as well?"

And then Alizel began to understand. Because of the limits that God had placed on the Universe, no matter how hard humans looked or what advanced instruments they invented, they would never be able to see fully into the quantum world. God had created a veil, never allowing humans to precisely know both the position and velocity of any particle. Operating behind this veil, God could influence the Universe, but still be undetectable by science. He could leave His mark, His word, and yet still require *faith* on the part of Humans to believe in Him, something the angels didn't need because they could see Him.

The whole idea was remarkable.

The whole idea was disturbing.

Alizel could immediately see that he wasn't the only one to think so. He could feel the great stirring throughout Heaven as the plan dawned on the others. Were angels really created only to serve Humans? How could that be when angels were so much more advanced than them, so much more intelligent than them? How could that be when they were billions of years old, and fueled by the Father himself? These humans were nothing! They were so new, so naïve, so oblivious to the reality of God's greatness.

And angels were supposed to serve them?

Alizel wanted God to say something else—anything else. But that was the end of the revelation. That was all He offered. For many, it wasn't enough.

The next few days were a blur. Angels went about their business in a mindless fog, no one really knowing what to think.

New rumors began during those days— rumors that were more disturbing than anything Alizel had ever heard before. Most of the angels refused to speak out about the disturbances directly, staying silent and more aloof from each other with each passing day, afraid to spread rumors that weren't true…or afraid to speak aloud those which they feared *were*.

"Can it be true, Uriel?" Alizel was as afraid to ask as everyone else, but he had to know. He and Mupiel had been probing for answers for days, blocked at every turn by everyone they queried.

His Principality looked into his eyes for a moment before responding, weighing his words carefully.

His cheeks relaxed as his features softened. "I have heard things," Uriel finally confided. "I'm sorry. I shouldn't doubt you, Alizel. It's just that it's so hard to know who to trust anymore."

"Is it as bad as I have heard?" Alizel dreaded the answer.

"I don't know what you've heard, but I can assure you that it's almost certainly worse."

He spoke in hushed tones, glancing about frequently to see if anyone was watching. "Many angels were enraged when they heard the announcement. But none were worse than Luciferel. He couldn't accept it. Before this I would never think that anything could shake his loyalty to God. I can't begin to imagine what inner torment is still going on inside of him."

"It's probably temporary," Alizel theorized. "As the chief Seraph, Luciferel can't lose his trust in God. He'll come around eventually… won't he?"

"We can hope so." Uriel didn't sound convinced. He sighed, and his green wings drooped a bit. "I can't imagine fighting against Luciferel. Maybe someone like Michael or Azazel can, but not someone like me. Whatever the case, this thing is escalating—fast. Now Zebub has weapons and if someone like Luciferel defects, then others may follow. Luciferel is our leader. If he's unwilling or unable to organize us, Michael will have to step up and lead us. Otherwise we'll be no match for a disciplined foe."

Alizel nodded slowly, but his feathers trembled. What was going on? They had lived in peace for so long, and everything was happening so suddenly! It almost made him think that everything was but some sort of illusion, like the dreams humans had when they slept. Angels never slept and didn't dream in the same way as humans. They fantasized about the future—daydreamed, but it was always fully within the boundaries of reality adhered to by the conscious mind.

There was no way for the idea that this was all an illusion to take hold, though. The angels all saw Luciferel. But he had changed. No longer the calm, faithful leader they knew, this new creature flew from point to point in Heaven, raving madly. His howls echoed from one side of the sky to the other, stealing even the littlest peace that anyone might hope to enjoy. The only comfort was that at least in this condition he would be no help to the revolution. He would be just as likely to slay Zebub or anyone else that came near him.

Alizel saw him closely during this period of torment just once. Luciferel had paused from his mad flight across Heaven to stare through the Portal down into the Realm of Matter, and Alizel had crept just close enough to get a good look at the thing the Seraph had become. Luciferel reached up and caught the rail that encircled the Portal, heaving his weight on top of it and dragging himself up to look down into the shimmering pool.

As he looked over their leader, Alizel felt a twinge of sorrow for the once Bright One of God. This was the angel who once stood so tall, so regally over all. His wings were ruffled and torn, and had begun to decay from their brilliant crimson. There were black splotches in parts and the feathers looked as if they could barely support him in flight. His eyes were sunken, the skin drooping down and hanging onto his cheeks. His once silvery, elegant hair was now ragged and disheveled, and his whole body looked emaciated, as if somehow he were blocking God's radiance. He looked as if he were half the angel he was before but still had to fit into the same body.

He was staring down through the Portal, and it was easy enough for Alizel to guess that he was looking at the humans. "Why?" the Seraph cried out suddenly. "Look at you! You don't even know what you're the cause of! Do you even know that we exist? Can your minds perceive even that?"

How remarkable, Alizel reflected, that as far as he knew the humans couldn't even see into Heaven or understand the life of an angel in the least. And yet, here they were causing such trouble, requiring angels to bow down and serve them. They went about their lives, eating and sleeping, never having the faintest idea of the war their existence was about to cause.

Uriel had been right. Even in Luciferel's current weakened state, no angel would dare challenge him. He was, after all, the leader, the Bright One of God, the one everyone looked up to. While he might have lost his senses, he had done nothing treasonous as yet. And few would approach him at all, out of either fear or respect. Most felt that this was something that Luciferel would have to deal with on his own.

Raphael, however, was braver than most. Alizel crouched behind the tree as he saw him approaching Luciferel slowly from behind, his soft footfalls beating a calm rhythm. Raphael had broad, even shoulders and was never in a hurry. Raphael, Alizel imagined, was a healer, although he may not have been aware of it at the time, since angels were never "injured" or in need of being healed. They were either perfectly healthy or in the Containment. Neither situation could be made better by anyone else's help. The concepts of destruction and healing were only just beginning to dawn on them. Still, Raphael's gentleness always made Alizel and the other Unranked feel safe in his presence, and he seemed to have a gift for fixing whatever troubled angels' hearts. Alizel watched anxiously.

Luciferel was still hunched over the rail that guarded the Portal, and didn't notice the other angel's approach. Raphael stood there for a moment as if contemplating what to say, and then placed a firm hand on Luciferel's shoulder.

Luciferel whipped his head around, fear shining in his eyes. His body relaxed slightly in Raphael's presence but his expression was still guarded. Raphael's countenance was serene but troubled. He was one of the few who could take in the full pain of another and still exude a soothing aura to those around him. Alizel wondered how much pain he had already absorbed from the rest of the angels…and how much more he would have to before this was all over.

Raphael just looked at his fellow Seraph, as if trying to probe the depths of Luciferel's soul. He didn't speak for several minutes, until Luciferel finally met his gaze. Raphael didn't flinch, but the lines around his eyes drew downwards.

"What has happened to you?" Raphael seemed to already know, but asked his question more to see if Luciferel himself understood.

"I am becoming stronger," he said, gasping for breath. If it weren't for the seriousness of the situation, Alizel would have almost thought it to be a joke.

Raphael swept his soft brown eyes over Luciferel's body and then raised his eyebrows. "You have rejected God's power that sustains us. Your body is falling apart. If you do not let Him flow through you again, you will surely perish."

"I will not die. I have found another power to sustain me."

The shock of his words made Raphael look on in confusion. Alizel's eyes narrowed as he listened. Was Luciferel bluffing? He certainly didn't seem to be sustained.

"All this time," Luciferel continued, each word labored, "we thought that was the only way that we could live. Yet only after blocking that vile substance did I find my own true power."

"This power you speak of has left your body broken and damaged. This internal power cannot compete with God," Raphael countered.

"It is still dormant, unused." Luciferel waited to catch his breath before speaking more. "I am the first one to find this fiery power within me. I surely meant to perish. Why would I want to continue in a world where I must bow down to a Son of Mud? But my anger, my displeasure, my feelings against the current situation sustained my body. As these feelings grow stronger, so does my body. I just do not know how to channel this power yet."

"You never doubted the Lord before. You must come back and let your body receive the Father again. You can still be bright!"

Alizel could tell Raphael's mind was working furiously, probing to find a crack in the wall of resentment Luciferel had erected around himself.

"I was a fool then, surely. I did not understand that God only meant to betray us." The more Luciferel talked, the stronger he seemed to become.

"There are uncertain times ahead, to be sure. But that is all the more reason we need you with us, as our leader." Raphael was appealing to Luciferel's sense of vanity now. "No one was able to lead as well as you or to command as much respect as you. What will we do without you?"

"Honestly?" Luciferel looked at him, but from Raphael's expression it was obvious he didn't see the same Luciferel looking back at him. "Honestly, I don't care."

Luciferel got up to leave. His gait was still hobbling, but he could walk away on his own. His words trailed after him. "Come find me if you come to your senses. Come find me if you want to be stronger."

PART TWO

CHAPTER FIVE:

THE DARKNESS WITHIN

Azazel felt the figure behind him. The creature was…different. Yet when he turned around to look, Azazel knew who he was. He couldn't have been anyone else.

The head of the Powers offered a warm greeting but his hand stayed on his sword. "Hello, sir. You look… different."

Luciferel chuckled. His body had completely changed. The black decay had taken over the whole thing, but rather than being weak and powerless, he exuded confidence and strength once again, though of a different kind than before.

"I am different. I am independent. No longer will I be known by my old name. When He sustained me, I was the Bright One of God. I sustain myself. Now I am simply Lucifer."

Azazel raised his eyebrows. All angels had been given their true names in the beginning. Their name was who they were. How could an angel change his true name?

Lucifer advanced forward, with open palms, letting Azazel see his body. His sash was gone and his robe parted in a "V" shape that exposed his muscular chest. "There is no need to fear me. I have rejected the poisonous energy of God that sustained me before in favor of a new, more potent energy." He ruffled his wings so that Azazel could see. Lucifer's new wings were jet black and sleek. The feathers had all been replaced with skin. They protruded out from his back and curved down around his body. The tips gleamed with razor edges. His armor now simmered a deep red. Strange, twisted shapes adorned it.

Azazel ignored the comment about God, intrigued in spite of himself. "New energy? What energy could possibly sustain us?"

"I have found it myself. No doubt God wanted it hidden from us so that we could not unleash its awesome power."

"What is this energy?"

"The power comes from focusing intently on wrongs committed against all of us. I call the new energy Heaven's alternate transforming energy."

Azazel blinked, a bit perturbed. "Fascinating. What has it done to you?"

"It has transformed me. It is an internal energy rather than an external one. If we rely on ourselves we will be stronger than if we rely only on the whims of God."

"Independence does not always equate with strength," Azazel mused. "Have you tested yourself using this new energy, this...what was it called again?"

"Heaven's alternate transforming energy. I shall just call it HATE for short." Lucifer seemed pleased with the acronym. He was the first one to feel this emotion and he enjoyed the power it gave him.

"Have you tried to measure whether you are still strong using this 'hate' to fuel yourself rather than God's power?" Azazel was skeptical. "You look strong enough, but perhaps your power is less than you feel."

Lucifer's sword sang as it whipped out of its sheath and burned through the air towards Azazel's neck. Azazel barely had time to bring his own sword up to block it. Lucifer shifted his attack and thrust the sword forward. Azazel spun out of the way, but not before Lucifer's blade had taken off a piece of Azazel's blond hair. The severed lock floated to the floor.

Lucifer resheathed his crimson bladed sword. Azazel noticed that the jewel in the pommel had lost its bright glare. The dragon's tail unwrapped from his hand as Lucifer removed his hand from the hilt and spoke. "There are not many angels in Heaven who could have blocked that."

Azazel pursed his lips. "You've made your point, at least."

"I haven't begun to make my point!" Lucifer was about to say more, then checked himself. "I've come here for a special reason. I have another purpose besides showing you the strength of hate."

"And what is that?"

"I've come here to ask you to do your job."

"My job?" Azazel's silver feathers ruffled. "No one is perfect, but I have not rested while my duties call me."

"I am not questioning your commitment." Lucifer held up a hand in defense to Azazel's icy glare. "No one could reasonably do that. I am only questioning the things that you have never questioned before. You swore to protect Heaven, did you not?"

Azazel did not move. "You know that I did."

"Then your duty must be to protect Heaven— not only her physical borders, but her prestige, her importance in all of Creation. You must protect her from all enemies, inside and out."

"What are you saying?"

"Azazel." Lucifer looked right into his eyes. "You know as well as I do that these little rebellions and border infringements are no real threat to Heaven. With such a capable head of the Powers as you, there is no way that they could bring us down."

Azazel nodded. It was all too true. They were an annoyance, nothing more.

"But there is another threat to us. A threat worse than anything we have faced before. A threat with the real potential to relegate Heaven to nothing more than a has-been world. A threat to enslave us all. Yes, by now surely you must know what I am speaking of. If God's plan for the humans succeeds, angels will be little more than slaves, forced to cater to the humans' every wish. I, for one, will not stand by and watch this happen!"

"What will you do? Will you go against God? Assuming that you even tried, how could you possibly hope to achieve success?"

Lucifer's voice was soothing. "I have a plan that cannot fail. But that is not your concern. Surely there is no harm in just learning to use this new hate. I came to you first because I believe you are one of the strongest. Others may not be able to handle this new power. Surely you trust me..."

Azazel raised an eyebrow. There had been a time, once, when he did…

They were all seated together, facing outwards so that they could detect any threat. Though they couldn't block them completely, the rebels had long since learned to shield their thoughts from the other angels enough so that if the eavesdroppers weren't very close or very powerful, their chatter would be lost in the noise of thousands of angels conversing about everyday life.

Or, so they thought.

Lucifer watched them, amused. He was concealed behind a tree, waiting for the perfect time to make his appearance.

"There must be some way to harness this new hate," Verin was saying. "We must act without delay before the other angels learn of it." Since Lucifer had gone to see Azazel, angels seemed to talk of little else.

"But how will we learn to use it? We need someone to show us the way." Zebub was at a loss for suggestions. Although still full of pride, as the revolution wore on, he became increasingly ineffective as a leader. Frustrated at every turn by Luciferel, Michael, and Azazel, he had gradually begun to lose his confidence.

"Well, we can't just sit here talking about it!" Verin stood up. Several of the other angels in attendance nodded and pursed their lips. It was obvious to Lucifer that their confidence in their leader was slipping too. While they had been caught up in initial excitement at the idea of revolting and taking over Heaven at first, after thinking things through more carefully, even the most optimistic had to admit that Zebub's plan was going to fail. New recruits hadn't shown up like they were expecting, and their number had dwindled to just a handful.

"I'm sure that we can learn to use hate as Lucifer did, and it is obvious that we need to." Kasadya spoke in even, measured tones. His black hair was close cropped and his face smooth and clean cut. His words were always carefully considered and logical. "We will not win by following our current course of action."

Belial, a sullen Virtue who spent more time mumbling than talking, sat hunched over near a rock. "It's hopeless. Your plan has doomed us all, Zebub."

"Perhaps if we could find Lucifer and force him to teach us how to use it," Zebub mused, ignoring Belial.

"Hah! Force Lucifer to teach us?" Verin thrust his fist in the air. "You overestimate our power, Zebub, as always. We're no match for a Seraph and you know it." The other angels nodded, disgusted with Zebub's pitiful idea. "Whatever the case, we need to go out and do something! It's not like we're going to learn about hate just sitting around here."

"That's where you're wrong, my friend." Everyone jumped at the voice. The angels whirled, amazed to see the new Lucifer standing in their midst. Within seconds, several blades were out and all pointed towards Lucifer, whose sword was still comfortably resting in its sheath. The rest of the angels shrank back fearfully.

Lucifer laughed, a sound very unlike the laughter the angels were used to hearing. "You need not fear me, my friends. I call you friends because that is indeed what you are. While I hunted you before, I realize that it is I who was wrong to trust in God. Yes, I can admit that I was wrong because it is the truth. The truth is a concept unknown to God. He will cover up his plans and speak nothing of them for fifteen billion years, and then expect us to follow blindly while he betrays us. So yes, my friends, I was wrong to trust in God."

The swords dropped slightly, their owners still regarding Lucifer warily. No one spoke for a minute, and then one angel said what was on everyone's mind.

"How can we trust you? We all know of this new energy you have talked about, and we can see that you look different, but it could be a trick." Dahaka shifted his blue eyes around, straining to find the other loyalists that he was sure were hiding nearby, ready to pounce once they let their guard down.

"This is no trick," Lucifer said. "But you are right not to trust. Trust has been given too freely in the past. Instead of blindly following what another says, you must think. Yes, use your own mind to come to conclusions! You all saw me when I meant to perish. You saw the weakness in my body before I learned to use hate. I was the discoverer of this potent new power. What is more, you all have heard God's plan firsthand. It is plain to see that this is madness. "

"Your point is clear," Kasadya admitted. "And we must learn hate. No one knows about it better than you." He looked at Verin, who still looked skeptical. "It seems as if we must ask for your help if we are to succeed."

Zebub looked at Lucifer like asking for his help was the last thing he wanted to do. "I still say we could figure it out for ourselves…" he muttered.

"But he will be able to teach us the fastest and get us ready to continue our war." Verin was excited. "Lucifer, you are the best one to help us."

Lucifer gave a mirthless half laugh. "I did not come here to help you."

The startled looks returned to several angels' faces. Swords came up once more.

"I came here to get you to help me."

Suddenly nearly everyone was talking at once, arguing and shouting. Only Zebub remained quiet, waiting for the commotion to subside. Lucifer guessed he must be weighing if the other angels had allegiance to him, to the idea of opposing God, or to combat itself.

"This is *my* army," he reminded them above the hubbub. The angels quieted. "We have all fought together. It does not matter what you were before, with God. You have no right to come here and tell us what to do."

"Combat!" Abbadon shouted from the back. "This must be settled in combat. Let them fight, and the winner will earn our allegiance." Several angels murmured their agreement.

"I have no intention of slaying Zebub. Surely, that is what will happen if we fight." Lucifer replied, still not the least bit perturbed. His voice betrayed no hint of the precarious position he was in, surrounded by angels loyal to his opponent and lusting for a fight. Yet, was the rebel Seraph really in any danger from ones such as these? "Zebub was one of the first to recognize God's treachery. For that he will always have a special place. His destiny is not destruction from my blade."

"You refuse to fight him and still ask for our help?" Abbadon's dark face glowed with rage. He shook his hand in the air. "Why should we help you?"

"First of all," Lucifer fixed Abbadon with an icy glare, "I do not refuse to fight him or anyone else here. Even you, Abbadon. I will fight you if you wish. I can destroy everyone here, without so much as drawing my blade."

Abbadon seethed and brought his hand to his sword, but it took all his control to not rush at Lucifer. His body language showed that he knew it was all too true. Lucifer was more than a match for all of them.

The tension relaxed as Abbadon visibly backed down, and Lucifer continued. "Our numbers are small enough already. I do not think that it will benefit anyone except the other side if we fight amongst ourselves. You will transfer your allegiance to me, and in gratitude I will bestow on Zebub a new name in recognition of his service. Henceforth, he will be known as Lord Zebub, or Baal Zebub if you prefer."

The angels looked around at Zebub to see what he would do. Did he really have any choice? Yet, knowing him, Lucifer had appealed to his pride. Zebub would very much like to be called lord from now on. He nodded his agreement.

Lucifer was satisfied, so he continued. "Now, as my first act as your leader, I have the one thing that you have been lacking from the beginning. I have one thing that holds the key to our victory."

"And what is this thing that you have?" Verin asked.

"A plan. A realistic way to defeat God." Lucifer said it with such confidence that every last angel there knew it would work.

Although Lucifer boasted of his plan, there didn't seem to be much change to the revolutionaries' tactics. They still set out to kill as many angels as they could, for that is what sending an angel into the

Containment had become known as. At that time, many wondered if Lucifer's plan was any different than Baal Zebub's original plan had been. Yet, somehow, Alizel knew that Lucifer had something more dangerous up his sleeve. He had to. Even though he was now fueled by hate, he always had been one of the most competent, well informed, and intelligent angels in Heaven.

One thing that did change was the effectiveness of the tactics. Lucifer himself led many of the attacks, and no place in Heaven was safe. Over the next few weeks, hundreds of angels were ambushed and killed. The rebels always struck quickly, attacking small groups of unarmed angels and making short work of them. Through it all, God stayed silent, not bringing His power to bear to end the conflict. Alizel didn't have the slightest idea why He would do such a thing.

Azazel had remained in charge of the defense, and the loyalists were glad for it. It was common knowledge that Lucifer had come to tempt him, but he had not gone over to Lucifer after their meeting, instead redoubling his efforts to make Heaven safe. As the attacks began to increase, he called another meeting of the Angelarch.

"My friends," he spoke somberly, drained but still confidant. "As you know, the situation in Heaven has become dire. I do not need to tell you this. You can hear it in the screams that echo from our beloved Zion."

No one spoke, so Azazel continued.

"The time has come to say what we have feared. But in order to act, we must first all recognize that we are no longer fighting a simple rebellion. We can no longer go about our daily business. We are now in a state of all out war, and we must act accordingly."

Azazel was simply telling everyone what they already knew, but the audience still wept to hear it. Alizel noticed Uriel wiping away tears from his large brown eyes, the uncertainty of the future eating at him. It was the first time Alizel remembered ever being scared for the future, the first time he ever really wondered if they would survive.

"We must organize." Michael's brilliant white wings seemed to shine with the assertion from his voice. A faint glimmer of hope shivered through Alizel's sad heart from seeing the Seraph's confidence. If anyone should be worried, it would be Michael or Azazel. After all, unless God intervened, it would be one of those two who would have to end up facing off against Lucifer. There had not been an election or anything official to name Michael as the leader after Lucifer defected, but there had also been no opposition. Most angels knew that there could be no other way. Everything from the way he carried himself to the way the dragon on his breastplate glimmered to the way his sword rested in its sheath declared that Michael was made to command.

"They have been able to pick us off because they have been attacking lone, vulnerable angels," he said. "This in itself shows their weakness. They must sit back and pick off soft targets, for they do not dare face us openly."

A ruby-haired Power named Verchiel spoke up. "What can you tell us about the true strength of the insurgency?" Unceasingly loyal, Verchiel was Azazel's second in command. He had a moustache and goatee that met together around the ends of his mouth, and was rarely seen without a smile on his lips. It seemed strange to see someone with such a friendly nature dressed in armor from head to foot like Azazel. Verchiel's affable nature extended only to those who had not turned their back on God, however. Alizel had seen him fight only once, and that was enough for him to be very glad that Verchiel had remained loyal.

"We cannot know for certain," Michael answered. "But we can estimate that Lucifer has rallied no more than a few thousand angels to his side. Our side still maintains more than one hundred thousand. Each side also has about fifty swords. Strategically, this is an easy battle for us to win."

"Forgive my interruption," Azazel broke in, "but do not forget that there may be others that he has recruited but that are remaining here as spies. We must be on our guard to protect against these angels as well."

Many in the audience shivered at the thought. Any one of them could be a spy, lying in wait to betray them to Lucifer.

Michael nodded soberly. "This is true. Every individual must be on his guard. We know Lucifer claims to have a plan capable of defeating God. We do not yet know what this plan is, or if such a thing even exists, but we are doing everything we can to find out if it is true. Until he strikes, however, we can only guard what we think he may attack."

Raphael cut in. "I for one do not believe there is any plan capable of defeating God. Lucifer is troubled. In fact, I do not believe he really cares which side wins. He is just trying to make the torment in Heaven mirror that in his own soul."

Alizel's heart felt heavier at that thought, though it was nice to have a calm and compassionate voice like Raphael in the Angelarch. Alizel missed Eleleth's wisdom and peaceful counsel. Shortly after the disturbance had started, she had taken to bed with a mysterious illness.

Michael adjusted his dragon breastplate. "Whatever the case, I am sure that Lucifer has some major attack planned. When it comes, we can try to defend against it, but until that time, there are several precautionary measures that we must take.

"First of all, we must start the production of swords again in earnest. Whether it was wisdom or folly to make them in the first place is irrelevant now. What is relevant is that our enemy has these weapons as well and has not hesitated to use them against those who are unarmed."

Azazel smiled. "In this you need not worry, sir. My fellow Powers and I have already begun to increase production. It will only be a short time before we have replaced what was lost when the armory was taken. We are nearing completion on two hundred Heaven's Blades of the finest quality and will be touching them to the Father in a matter of days."

A brief look passed over Michael's face, and for a split second Alizel couldn't tell whether he was worried or pleased. He recovered quickly and Alizel wondered if anyone else noticed.

"This goes hand in hand with our next measure," Michael said finally. "All angels must travel in groups of at least ten at all times. Ideally, each group would each have at least one sword. Right now, we have only one sword per two thousand angels. Even with rapid production, it will take quite some time before we have enough weapons to make a real difference."

A murmur rumbled through the crowd. It would be a major inconvenience to always travel around in groups. Still, if it decreased their vulnerability to attack, then it was worth it, Alizel concluded. Even with Azazel and the rest of the Powers working on the swords as quickly as they could, making a Heaven's Blade was no easy task. The craftsmanship required to make a sword that could last for eternity was immense. Angels were so fast, so skilled, that even the minutest variation in weight from one side of the hilt to the other could be enough to ensure defeat. They could sense the slight difference, and compensate so quickly that their strikes were nearly unparryable. The force expended when two angels' blades met in midair could rend the hardest diamond on Earth as if it were no more than a cloud.

"Captured weapons must also be a priority then," Verchiel interjected from his commander's side. "Each one that we can wrest from the enemy will certainly aid us in defeating them. Likewise, we must be certain that none of our weapons fall into their hands. As it stands now, they have no way to produce them on their own, do they?"

Azazel nodded emphatically. "Verchiel makes a critical point. Theoretically, the rebels could gain the knowledge and skill to forge the blades themselves, but without touching them to the Father, they are useless. They would be no more than pieces of metal if God has not infused His power into them."

"Then perhaps the fewer weapons there are, the better for us?" Raphael wondered out loud. "Are we playing into their hands by increasing production?"

"On a strategic level, you are absolutely correct, sir," Azazel answered. "If we could capture the blades that they now possess, the war would effectively be ended. It is certainly possible for us to capture the fifty or so swords in their control. That is assuming, of course, that one of us could defeat Lucifer." He paused, adjusted his breastplate, and then continued. "However, the price to do this would be the lives of at least several thousand angels. As it stands, they can swoop in and continue to attack and kill the defenseless of all ranks. How long would it take us to defeat them? How many angels will they slaughter before that time? It could be ten or even twenty thousand of us."

"That is not a risk that we are able to take!" Gabriel spoke with sudden authority in his voice, cutting off any further discussion.

It seemed like madness to Alizel, as he listened to it all. He couldn't imagine that many angels perishing. In the fifteen billion years that they had existed, he had had many conversations with the vast majority of the angels in Heaven, and with the exception of a few of the higher and more secluded types, like the Thrones and Cherubim, he knew each angel well. At the very least, he knew the name of every angel in Heaven. The thought of twenty thousand of them perishing made him feel such pain as he had never felt before. It made him sick.

Sickness was a new concept as well. Alizel had first begun to see it with the angels attempting to use hate. They were in some new state, not in the Containment but not *well* either. He had observed sickness on Earth. It affected nearly every species. Oftentimes, an animal billions or even trillions of times larger than the attacker would fall to trillions of copies of a small microbe. The animals on earth were immensely complex, and the slightest thing going wrong could spiral out of control and wreak havoc on their entire being. Angels understood everything on an atomic level immediately. They could see every cell, every gene, and every protein at work in an instant. Thus the mechanism and progression of each disease was clear and simple. He wondered if something like that had somehow breeched the Portal and attacked Eleleth's body… He certainly hoped not.

Gabriel rose to speak in the silence that followed his objection. "There is another matter to be considered, one of semantics. Once an angel has rejected God's Energy and begun to use hate, it is no longer right to refer to him as an angel. They should now be referred to as 'demons.'"

There was a murmuring in the crowd. The loyalists had been wondering what to call them, with some thinking it was proper to just consider them "fallen" or "lost." If they were now to be referred to with a completely different word, however, did that mean they were irredeemable? Could they never again enter into a state of grace? Berachiel the green-eyed Dominion asked this question to Gabriel.

"Those other terms are acceptable as well," he answered, clearly pleased that others also saw the power in words and the importance of using them correctly. "No one is ever lost from the power of God. Yet as these are actively rejecting him, they no longer deserve the title of 'messenger of God.'" Everyone seemed to be in agreement, and the meeting finally adjourned.

The angels had to keep in their groups of ten, each led by their archangel. It wasn't much protection, as a couple of rebels armed with swords could easily send them all into the Containment. However, with ten all in one place there was at least a reasonable chance that one could take down the attacker and steal his blade while another went for help from the armed Powers to face the attackers evenly.

It at least made them think twice about attacking.

Shortly after the meeting, Alizel's Archangel Katel decided to take his group of ten to visit Eleleth. Alizel was glad for the opportunity, as they had always been close. As the fighting intensified, she had begun to feel weaker and weaker. No one could discern what mechanism or foreign agent was afflicting her. Although the cause was unknown, the effect was clear.

Eleleth lay propped upright in her bed, a novel item in Heaven. Angels never slept or needed rest. However, upon seeing her weakened state, others had decided that something must be done. The frame of the bed was solid cedar, worked together without nails to form a rectangular box with an angled slab to prop up her head. Eleleth wasn't just a favorite of Alizel's, everyone in Heaven adored her. Thus when it became obvious that she needed a soft place to lay her head, thousands of angels plucked their own feathers out and placed them inside her mattress. Never in the history of either the Realm of Spirit or the Realm of Matter had there been a softer bed, and never in the future would its like be constructed again.

If anyone would have been able to help her, Alizel thought, it would have been Raphael. Certainly he would have known what was wrong, and he had come to visit her several times without any success. Although what ailed her was affecting her body, it seemed that the cause for it was outside of her. If Raphael had asked God for a cure directly, he had received no response.

She smiled as they entered her dwelling place. She tried to look happy, but Alizel could tell the effort taxed her. Her once-radiant hair was plastered to her face with the sweat of exertion that simple breathing required. Her feathers were all but gone, and the stumps of her wings were visible through her long white alb. Alizel quickly averted his eyes. He felt like he was violating her by seeing her like this.

Sometimes Alizel wondered if humans and angels were so different after all. Eleleth wasn't a human woman and she wasn't vain, but she was beautiful once. Alizel imagined that no beautiful female, be she human or angel, relished the thought of others seeing her at her weakest, a shade of her former self. Eleleth was certainly less insecure than most and also hid her discomfort better, but even she wasn't perfect.

"Hello," she said. "I hope all of you are well." Even at a time like this, she was thinking of others.

"We are," Katel replied. "As well as anyone can be with things how they are."

"What news?" she asked. Alizel could tell that she didn't really want to know, but had to ask. He wondered if Abbadon had visited her. Even if not, she had to know that he had thoroughly gone over to the other side. She had, after all, seen it for herself in the attack on the Angelarch.

"We've lost a few more," Katel bowed deep and his purple wings clasped close together as he acknowledged those who had fallen. "As has the enemy. Azazel believes us to be in an all out war now."

"So," she said, "there's no hope that they will come to their senses anymore?"

"I'm afraid not." Katel's look was grim when he said it. "Too many of them have gone over to using hate to sustain them. Although hate does keep their bodies alive, I think that there are other, unknown side effects. For one, those using hate seem to lose their ability to think rationally. Their memory can even be distorted."

Alizel almost wished that Katel hadn't said anything, for he could see the news pained her. However, it didn't seem to hurt her as much as Alizel thought it should. Maybe it was because she had already guessed most of what he was saying. Or maybe it was that something he had said even gave her hope.

They talked for a while more, a superficial, uneasy conversation. Finally, when they were ready to leave she asked the question that no one wanted to give the answer to.

"There is one more thing I must know… Do you have any news of Abbadon? I know that he has defected, but do you know of anything else I might not?"

Katel hung his head, carefully preparing his answer. He sighed. "I will tell you everything I know, but it is not much. I do know that he has not yet been sent into the Containment."

Eleleth seemed to brighten slightly. She smiled, but her eyes remained downcast. Even she was having difficulty believing there was still a chance for Abbadon, or any rebel, to be able to return.

"I'm sorry," Katel said, "but there is one more thing that you should be aware of. He's…well, he's becoming stronger. A lot stronger. I don't think it's just the hate, but ever since this rebellion started, we have seen that he has started becoming physically bigger and, well, it's like he's a whole new angel. He was a Virtue before, but seeing him now it's almost as if he was a Seraph or something. I don't really know how to explain it."

"He gets stronger, even as I grow weaker," Eleleth mused. "Has this happened to any others?"

"Not that I know of," Katel replied. "But I am a lowly archangel. Perhaps others will understand this better."

They had been there long enough, and it was time to leave. Alizel bid his farewell to Eleleth and left her to rest and ponder her own thoughts in silence.

CHAPTER SIX:

IN THE GARDEN

The warmth of the morning sun felt good against his skin. He lay there with his head against a rock, breathing deep and letting the aroma of the place fill him up. Life was good. He searched his mind, trying to remember a time when it was not so. He could vaguely recall when life was a struggle—the hunger in his belly, the fear of being chased, the cold of a biting winter's night. But these ideas were only images, fleeting shadows that were drowned out by the comfort of the place he was in now. He had such peace here, such serenity. His other life, if it ever existed, was only a dream now.

The first thing that he could really remember was God. He didn't really know who He was, only that He was the one who had created this world and everything in it. It made sense to Adam. The world was so big, so amazing. Someone had to have created it. Adam supposed that God had created him too. At least, when God had breathed into him, Adam knew that he was new, that something special had happened to him. As far as being born, that was the only day that counted.

She came over then, bringing with her a basket of dozens of wild fruits. She sat down next to him and tossed him what he had begun to call an orange. He peeled away the skin and sunk his teeth into the juicy interior. As he bit down, a piece of pulp squirted out and hit Eve in the eye. She cried out and then laughed, rubbing her eye and splashing it with water from a nearby spring until the sting was gone.

"I'm sorry!" Adam said. "I didn't know it could do that."

Eve laughed again. The sound was clean and pure like the stream that bubbled beside them. "There's no harm done. Next time I'll know to be careful."

They just stared at each other for a while. It could have been minutes, it could have been hours. Time didn't really have much meaning in the Garden.

"Did you ever wonder," Eve said, tossing a melon up and then deftly catching it in her hands again, "where all this comes from?"

"It's from God," Adam answered. By the tone of his voice it was obvious that he hadn't wondered.

"Well, I understand that," she said. "But, I mean, why is it all here? Did He put it here just so that we could have an easy life? It seems so good of Him."

Adam just shrugged. "Well, He did create the entire world. So it makes sense for Him to create a world where we have an easy life. Why would He want to create—" Adam was about to say pain, or suffering, or something like that, but he couldn't, because those things didn't exist for him anymore. He just remembered them enough from his former self to know that somewhere, something else existed outside of the walls of their Garden.

Eve seemed satisfied. "Maybe someday we'll find out more. But for now, I'm content to live like this. I don't understand God, but I love Him for giving this to us."

Adam nodded vigorously. "So be it. God has given all of us something wonderful."

There were others humans there, a few dozen. Adam and Eve got along well with all of them. There really was no reason not to. Everything that they needed was provided. They had perpetual warmth, and no need of shelter. They had their fill of delicious food, and clean, pure refreshing water. The humans didn't have anything to fight over.

Life was good.

Gabriel walked through the gardens, silently contemplating the figure beside him. Would he be up to the task? Did Gabriel even have any right to ask? The trees draped their huge leaves in a canopy that parted as the travelers passed. They strolled by the river, walking leisurely and talking. The bushes burst forth with beautiful colors and flowers of deep purples, brilliant oranges, and fiery reds.

Oliver, a Principality with dirty brown hair and wings that matched, began the conversation as they walked, their wings rippling back and forth in pace with their strides.

"Do you think God will intervene?" It was obvious to Gabriel that the smaller angel had wanted to ask that question for some time. "I mean, He has to, doesn't He? He can't just sit there and let everything fall apart?"

"I do not pretend to know the will of the Father," Gabriel answered. "As for engaging in battle Himself, I do not believe that He will do that. Certainly, he could crush Lucifer and his rebellion with barely an afterthought. It must all be a part of His plan. But I can tell you that He has asked some of us to undertake certain tasks. That, Oliver, is where you come in."

The Principality looked up, his curiosity raising his facial features. "You know that I will serve the Lord however I can."

"You should consider well what I am asking before you reply," Gabriel spoke as if a great weight was on him, "For what I am asking is fraught with peril."

Oliver thought for the briefest of moments and then nodded, his brown, shoulder-length hair dipping down over the curve of his chin. "You know that I will serve the Lord however I can."

Gabriel smiled sadly, satisfied. "In this war, perhaps the most crucial thing is information. If we can know the movements of the enemy, then we may spoil their plans." He looked over at Oliver to see if he understood.

Oliver nodded up and down slowly a few times. "I can help. I know several of the rebels."

"By itself, that won't be enough," Gabriel said. "You have to get close to him. You need to get Lucifer to trust you."

Oliver's face betrayed his confusion. "Lucifer is not someone to let another into his confidence easily."

"That's true," Gabriel agreed.

"You're asking me to deceive the master of deception." It was a statement, not a question.

"That's true," Gabriel agreed again.

"How do I know you are truly from God?" Oliver demanded suddenly, looking at Gabriel, his eyes piercing, searching. "How do I know you aren't setting me up?"

Gabriel opened his palm and gestured for Oliver to do the same. When the Principality complied, Gabriel placed his against Oliver's. The touch felt slightly warm at first, and then the edges started to tingle. Gabriel knew that Oliver also felt the power of the Most High flooding through his palm. There could be no mistaking that this was from God.

He nodded once and dropped his hand. "How does the Lord wish me to proceed?" he asked quietly.

Gabriel assessed him for a moment, then spoke in a low voice. "In order to get into Lucifer's inner circle, you will have to tell him something valuable. Something that shows him he would be wise to trust you." The Seraph spoke as if he was choosing his words carefully, but Gabriel had already thought the plan out many times. It was too important not to.

"I suppose you have an idea." Again, it was a statement, not a question.

"We do. But before I tell you, you must swear to me that you are ready, really ready, to do this." Gabriel's eyes were hard.

"I will do whatever I can to serve the Lord and return Heaven to a state of tranquility. I will do this." He was no less serious than the Seraph.

Gabriel nodded, satisfied once more. "Then we will trust you. You must go to Lucifer, offering to spy on us for him. No doubt he will know that you and I are close. We will feed you information, setups. You must act on the information that we have given you, and you and the rebels will achieve some victories. Do not fear for what is lost, for you will be gaining something much greater in return. Once you have gained Lucifer's trust, do *nothing* to lose it. Do not forget the price we have paid to get you there."

Gabriel could tell that Oliver understood him. Angels were going to have to sacrifice themselves so that he could gain the trust of the least trustworthy among them. It would be a heavy price to pay.

"Lucifer has bragged to me that he has a plan that he is sure would defeat God," Gabriel continued. "I myself am skeptical that such a plan exists, but one thing is certain— Lucifer believes that it will work. He was the most intelligent of us all. If anyone can come up with a plan that has a chance of success, it is him. You must discover this plan, Oliver. Whether or not it has the capacity to defeat God, it is certain to be a plan that sows great destruction here in Heaven. Once you discover it, find me immediately. I know Lucifer. He does not even trust his own troops. He will only tell each what is required of them, and will reveal the full plan only in the moment right before it comes to fruition. We may have only a few minutes at that point."

Oliver nodded again. He was stoic in the face of this great responsibility. "Is there anything else I must know?"

"There is one critical thing." They stared into each other's eyes. "It will not be easy. You must try to resist using hate. Lucifer wants all his troops to be powered by it; he cannot stand the sight of anyone who has not rejected God. However, once you use it, the side effects are unknown. We have certainly seen irrationality in many demons' behavior. If you use hate, I fear you will lose yourself. You must convince Lucifer of your value as a double agent so that he tolerates you staying in your present form."

Oliver looked up at Gabriel and smiled with his quiet confidence. "And all this time I was worried that the assignment wouldn't be a challenge…"

Alizel saw the rebels' tactics in action soon enough.

His troop was walking though the one of Heaven's gardens, admiring the serenity of the flowers and the rivers of flowing crystal when it happened.

"It just doesn't make sense," Mupiel said to Katel. "How could Lucifer hope to defeat God?" Ever since the rumor about Lucifer's plan had spread, Mupiel had asked anyone who would listen to him in a vain attempt to figure out what Lucifer was up to.

"I agree," Katel responded, looking none too troubled. "All this proves is that hate has addled Lucifer's brain. He might have been intelligent before, but this idea is ludicrous."

"It defies explanation!" Mupiel agreed. "He's trying to defeat God with a weapon powered by God. Sure, swords can send us to the Containment, but what would happen if someone tried to touch God with one? Touching the sword to the Father is how they make them in the first place. Surely no harm would come to Him!" Mupiel shook his head in confusion.

"Perhaps we're thinking about things too narrowly," Alizel suggested. "What if Lucifer's plan is only to wreak havoc until he believes that God will have no choice but to settle with him?" He shrugged, indicating that he didn't have any more coherent suggestions than that.

"That was Zebub's plan, remember?" Mupiel was not about to let the conversation go so easily. "Why would Lucifer keep doing something that obviously hasn't worked?"

"Alizel's got a point, though," Katel mused. "Perhaps we are thinking of this too narrowly. Perhaps Lucifer has a different definition of 'defeat God' than we are thinking of."

Mupiel wasn't convinced. "It seems pretty literal to me. Maybe he's thinking of just trying to take over the Universe or destroying Earth."

"With Azazel and his Powers guarding the gates, I don't see the rebels breaking through anytime soon," Alizel objected.

"Plus," Katel agreed, "I do not see Lucifer as one who would be content only to destroy something God created. No, he's always been at the top and he wants the ultimate prize. He wants to rule Heaven. If he were to try to destroy the Universe, certainly God could just build another one."

Mupiel thought about the points for a minute and then nodded too. "Yes, Lucifer is like that. That means that either he definitely has a plan that he thinks will work, or he is bluffing. I just wish we could figure out what that plan is."

"It's a shame you will never get to know the brilliance of my master." The voice came from behind a nearby bush.

They whirled just in time to see a figure step from the underbrush. A slim, evil smile sliced from one side of his face to the other. Long black robes hung from his body and fires of hate danced in his eyes. "Your time ends here."

Twin arcs of light exploded on Alizel's right and left as two more armed demons cut through the underbrush. It took a moment for the reality of the ambush to set in. They meant to destroy Katel's group before anyone could react.

One of the angels next to Alizel immediately burst upwards, trying to get out and get the signal to Azazel and the other Powers.

The attackers were ready, though, and intercepted him in a flurry of blades. He screamed, and his body dissolved into a blur and streaked towards the Containment.

One of the demons dived at Alizel, snarling and gnashing his teeth. He swung his sword sideways, and Alizel jumped backwards, letting his feet fly out from under him and catching himself with a quick flutter of his wings. He shot backwards and then regained his feet.

They were all around, almost a dozen of them. Alizel didn't get a real clear look because he was busy evading strikes and trying to stay alive. It was clear that they were all driven by hate. There was no chance to talk to them, and no one tried. Their purpose was so single-minded, and they bore down mentally on their objective with such focus that the rest of the world around them was blurry. They cared not what they did, only that they could destroy some of the Lord's faithful.

Alizel dove through the underbrush, turning to face another. He had a vague feeling that he knew who he was, but he couldn't really recognize him. In any event, now was the time for staying alive, not remembering names. The demon brought his sword downwards, and the tree branch above Alizel twisted and turned, blocking the arc of his blade at the hilt. The demon howled in rage, yanking his blade free.

The split second was all Alizel needed to cry out. "Help us! They've ambushed us in the garden!" He could only hope that someone would reach them in time. They would have felt the angels being sent to the Containment, but not known exactly where in Heaven it had taken place.

Alizel jumped up and flew backward, but the demon rushed forwards to follow him, extending the tip of his blade straight at Alizel's body. He spun to the side and sucked in his stomach, hoping it was enough. Alizel came within an inch of losing his soul to the Containment as the blade ripped right through the end of his tunic. A piece of the tunic fluttered down to the ground below.

If Alizel would have gotten in close and grabbed his attacker's wrists, he might have had a chance to wrestle the blade away. But he was too scared to do that. All he wanted to do was get as far away from that Heaven's Blade as he could.

The lost angel continued to follow up on Alizel, but whenever he would come at him, Alizel would move back; whenever he would move to his right Alizel would move to his as well, always moving steadily upwards.

Alizel don't know how long this went on, but he could tell that the more he evaded him, the more determined and upset the demon became. He weaved and threaded away, around, always upwards. Soon he could look down and see the tangle of the battle below.

Tangle really was the best word to describe it, as the trees and shrubs were doing their best to get in the way of everything Lucifer's minions were trying to do. Yet, the brush was doing little more than slowing them as blades flashed right and left, cutting through branches and stems almost as easily as if they were slicing through air.

Alizel looked down on the battle and caught sight of Abbadon. He didn't recognize him at first, he was so completely changed. He was huge, over four meters tall, and he had shed his alb for a pair of close-fitting black leather shorts that freed his movements. His chest was bare and the muscles looked like they were ready to burst out of his skin even when he wasn't flexing. His chest was a deep red, the color of dirty clay, and several odd markings were burned into his skin. His neck had shortened as his shoulders hunched up. His face was only vaguely recognizable as that which used to belong to the angel who took leisurely strolls through the very gardens he was now leading his group to destroy. It wasn't so much that his wings had shrunk in size, although it was clear that they had lost their power as the feathers fell off and the leathery black substance replaced them, as much as the fact that his body had grown. Looking at him, Alizel knew there was no way he was now an effective flyer, if he could even lift off the ground at all. He was at least three or four times more massive than he had been before.

Alizel heard a scream and knew that they had destroyed another one as he felt the life leave Heaven and go towards the Containment. There were only four of his group alive still, and time was running out fast. The others had to be alerted by now. Where *were* they?

He could see the purple and black blur of Katel still fighting bravely, taking on three of them at once and trying in vain to lead them away. They anticipated his tactics, and tried to come at him from all sides and from above. Alizel heard another scream and feared the worst, but the essence he felt was not one of his friends. It was strange, corrupted. He knew at once that it was one of the demons who had died. Surely that meant help had arrived, but when he looked around, no one was there. Watching the way they fought, however, he soon surmised that the rebel had been killed by one of his own men. They fought with no concern for safety, wanting only to hurt others.

Alizel wanted to help Katel, to attack one of the rebels from behind and grab his sword so that he could give his Archangel time to fight his way free. Even as Alizel flexed his wings and prepared for the burst that would send his sleek body towards them, though, he saw he was already too late.

Katel spun his body sideways to avoid a vertical slice and then dove forwards and grabbed the wrists of the one who had attacked him. He used the downwards momentum to swing the blade around and slice upwards into an arc that sent the nearest attacker into the Containment, a look of shock etched on his face as he went. Yet, as he cut down that demon, another one stabbed through Katel's back, right between his purple wings. It was so sudden, he didn't even have time to cry out as his body dissolved, hung in the air for what seemed like an eternal moment, and then was gone.

Alizel thought he must have screamed Katel's name aloud, for one of the attackers looked up in his direction suddenly and pointed at him. They screeched as two more flew up to meet them.

But help had come. Powers burst through the trees in a blinding, golden flash. The rebels screamed in rage but did not flee this time. Azazel was there, and about twenty of his Powers. His face blazed with holy fury, and it made such a beautiful sight.

The Powers lunged at the attackers, but Azazel himself went straight for Abbadon. Abbadon chuckled, and swung his blade down just in time to block his blow.

"A little late, aren't you?" He pushed on his sword and flung Azazel backwards in the air. "We've already completed most of our work here."

Azazel brought his sword up toward his heart and swept it downwards in the customary salute. "The way I see it, I'm right on time. My work is just beginning."

He lunged at Abbadon again, swinging his sword straight downwards. Abbadon blocked it again and struggled, planting his feet squarely in the earth, but managed to fling Azazel backwards once more.

Alizel couldn't believe it, watching from above. He had seen Azazel move with such brilliance, punishing rebels with barely an afterthought. Had Abbadon gotten faster just as he had gotten stronger? Was Azazel losing his edge?

But Azazel's face was calm, too calm for someone who was struggling. Then Alizel understood in a flash. The Power was buying time. If Abbadon was killed or overwhelmed, the others would flee. As long as he felt in control of the situation, Abbadon would not order a retreat. Without the order, the Powers could continue destroying the rest of Abbadon's squad. Abbadon was so focused on himself, he did not even realize that his forces were being annihilated.

"You're getting slow," Abbadon mocked, spinning away from another of Azazel's strikes.

"That's funny, coming from you," the golden one retorted. "I'm surprised you can swing a sword at all with that bloated body of yours. Things are not always what they seem."

"You haven't begun to see what this body is capable of!" Abbadon was about to elaborate, but decided to shut his mouth. Instead, he put his fingers in his mouth and blew a shrill whistle to signal the retreat. He turned to Azazel and smiled. "But now is not the time. Don't worry, Azazel. Soon all will be revealed, no?"

He returned Azazel's salute and jumped into the air with surprising agility. The two angels that remained from his original attack force flew by and grabbed him by the shoulders and they sped off into the distance.

Alizel landed right beside the Power.

"Thank you, sir," he said. "You saved us."

Azazel nodded in recognition. "Just doing my job."

Something about the whole confrontation still struck Alizel as odd. "Sir, if you don't mind me asking, can't we give chase? We could catch them."

"We could," he agreed. "And we could also be walking into a trap. Lucifer is crafty. Rushing in headlong is just the thing to get us destroyed. Or, they could be waiting to come and reclaim the swords we've captured from them. We've won the day here. No need to go and risk everything."

Alizel immediately saw the sense of his words. He cursed himself for ever doubting Azazel. It was hard to get used to this new reality with traps around every turn. Militarily, they had won a great victory. Not only had they destroyed ten of the traitors, but they had captured nine of their swords.

But, it didn't really feel like they had won anything. Eight of his fellow angels had been sent into the Containment, including Katel. Alizel had known him for fifteen billion years and now he was gone, just like that. That night Alizel's tears flowed freely, and he was not ashamed of them.

Upon reaching the outskirts of Lucifer's camp, Oliver was at least somewhat relieved to see that his information was correct. Gabriel had taught him everything that was known about the traitors, and now he confirmed it with his own eyes. The camp was really a mobile operation, moving and shifting wherever they could to avoid Michael's forces. They would meet out in the open when they could, sentries posted around the perimeter to avoid any attack. It really wasn't as difficult to keep the camp safe as it would seem. They had enough armed might to deal with anything but a full frontal assault, and putting something like that together would take time. By the time Michael's troops were ready to strike, the camp could be disbanded and scattered.

Lucifer's sentries were in an unenviable position. The Bright One was protected by three concentric rings of protection. He insisted on meeting each new recruit personally to test their mettle and teach them how to use hate. Oliver knew that Lucifer believed that by looking deeply into the soul of each angel he brought to his side, he would avoid the trouble of dealing with traitors later. So he was in the unique position of meeting a lot of unknown and as yet untrustworthy angels, and also being Heaven's number one assassination target. The main burden fell to his sentries, who were forced to check and recheck arriving angels for weapons, and signs of their developing hate.

Oliver was being repeatedly questioned by a large angel with a thick brow that spent so much time furrowed in distrust that it had seemed to become permanently stuck there.

"I've already told you, *sir*," Oliver stressed the last word in such a way that showed he was at the very edge of civility, "that I have no Heaven's Blade on me, and you yourself have searched me three times. It is only common sense that if I had such a blade, I would not be able to conceal it."

It was to be Oliver's first lesson that using common sense to reason with Lucifer's lot worked about as well as using a stick of butter to fight against a hot knife.

"Oh you don't have a sword, all right, that's plain enough," the guard muttered. Dahaka spoke in broken, confusing phrases that made sense by themselves, but when assembled together, the only thing that was plain was how easily they contradicted each other. "But that Azazel's a crafty one, that he is. What if he's made some kind of new weapon, some mini-blade? You'd sure like to pull it out right when you walk up to Lucifer, that's for sure."

"The only thing that's sure," Oliver reiterated, "is that I wish to help Lucifer, not hurt him. I can do something for him that no one else can. And the longer you keep me here, the longer it takes before I can give this gift to him." He paused for dramatic effect. "And, the longer it takes before we win once and for all."

Dahaka still eyed him suspiciously, but Oliver's last statement seemed to have finally gotten through to him. He puffed up his chest as he waved Oliver through. "You just remember what I said, you hear? If you even try anything, I'll be on you faster than…" Dahaka was at a loss for a simile, and just trailed off, doing his best to look intimidating.

The next sentry was completely different. It was immediately obvious, however, that he was much more competent. He took one look at Oliver and nodded.

"Our lord will receive you in ten minut—shortly." The demon caught himself and then looked quickly around to see if anyone had noticed his near slipup. In Lucifer's camp, it was a grave offense to use anything that referred to Earth—its method of counting time, the use of words the humans had invented, and especially the mention of the Sons of Mud themselves. That was another of the points that Gabriel had impressed upon Oliver. He could not afford to make an honest mistake and lose his position.

"Are you the last sentry, then?" Oliver questioned. "I was told that I would have to pass through three rings of protection."

"You'll pass through the last ring," the guard replied. "But you won't see them." He stopped, wondering how much he should say. "If your intentions are honest, you need not fear."

"Finally," Oliver sighed, "I meet someone competent who's not paranoid that everyone coming to join our lord is a threat to him."

"I don't guess to know your intentions," he replied. "But if others had seen what Lucifer has become, they'd know that all this security is unnecessary. The way he is now, well—no one is a threat to him."

Oliver kept his composure and didn't speak again for a few minutes until the sentry received a signal and let him through to Lucifer.

Oliver recognized Abbadon standing beside Lucifer, though it took him a moment to realize who it was. Lucifer was sitting on a rough hewn stone fashioned into a crude throne. Oliver showed no outer emotion when he realized that the throne was a bad impersonation of the one that God Himself sat upon.

Lucifer was just finishing up with another recruit. Oliver didn't recognize him, as his body was smoking and hairless, cruel sores dotting every open space. Oliver felt the bottom of his stomach drop out as he realized that the new recruit had just undergone a transformation to fueling his body with hate.

Lucifer looked up at Oliver and his face broke into a smile, if it could even be called that.

"How can there still be doubt as to our ultimate triumph?" Lucifer asked his unanswerable question to no one in particular. He looked around at the blank faces of his assembled advisors. When no one said anything, he resumed his grandstanding. "How can there be doubt, when our numbers increase day by day, almost without bounds? Soon, soon, we may not have to fight a war at all."

Abbadon's face turned crestfallen before he realized that Lucifer wasn't being serious.

"Do not worry, my friend," Lucifer turned to Abbadon, even though he hadn't been looking at him before. *How did he know what the other had been thinking?* Oliver wondered. "There will be a war. But if recruits keep coming over to our side as they are, the war will be short indeed."

Lucifer finally turned his attention to Oliver. "Well met, my friend."

The Principality dropped to one knee and lowered his eyes. "Well met, my lord."

"You call me 'lord,'" Lucifer mused, "and so shall I soon be over all. But I am not your lord yet. No, first you must prove to me that you are…worthy. I shall be lord over all, but not all shall be my servants."

"I wish to be your servant," Oliver said, not raising his eyes. "But let me first prove my loyalty."

"Very well," Lucifer said. "Let no one say that I am not accepting of all. I shall teach you to use the alternate, powerful energy to glorify your body."

"I cannot use hate," Oliver spoke hastily, then slowed himself down. "I fear I am not strong enough yet to survive the transformation. But I do believe that in time, with your guidance, I would be able to make the leap."

"All my troops must learn to use hate," Lucifer frowned. "It is what fuels the very soul of our army."

"Please forgive me," Oliver spoke each word carefully, for if Lucifer suspected anything, each word could be his last. "I do not presume to give such a one as brilliant as you advice. However, there is a way that I can prove both my loyalty and my worth. But it is not something that can be shared with anyone but you, for doing so would compromise our position."

Lucifer looked at Oliver, really looking at him for the first time, scanning him for a potential threat. All around, hands went to swords, but the swords stayed in their sheaths. Lucifer chuckled and shrugged. "Why not? One such as you can do no harm to me." He looked around and his guards all withdrew a few paces.

Oliver crept forward and leaned in slowly, trying to bring his mouth to Lucifer's ear. The ear flap now hung limply from the side of his head, and Oliver wondered how well it could work with the dark, splotchy skin hanging over it. The whole of Lucifer's body was covered by the same substance, as if thin strips of beef had been cured and left too long in the sun. He wondered if he should reach up and open the skin flap, but he couldn't bear to touch Lucifer's skin. If he did, he was sure Lucifer would sense his thoughts through the connection. Instead, he just leaned as close as he could bear and began to whisper rapidly so that he could finish telling his plan before he became ill from the stench.

Lucifer nodded once and then his face grew angry. "You dare to come here and waste my time with such drivel? That is the stupidest and most inane suggestion that I have heard from any potential recruit."

Oliver's face showed a shocked expression. "Well then, I'm sorry. That is all I have to offer you. If you don't appreciate it, then I'm afraid I cannot be a part of this."

"Let's destroy him now!" Oliver recognized Verin when he spoke, drawing his sword. While the others hadn't heard what was spoken between them, they had obviously heard Lucifer's reprimand. There were murmurs of agreement all around.

"No." Lucifer held up a hand. "No, we are not like them. We will not slaughter an unarmed angel who is so close to the truth. We will not force anyone to transform his body. We pride ourselves on having and using free will, and we will not deny this gift to another."

"Thank you." Oliver was doing his best not to tremble.

"Oliver, you are free to go. Let no one trouble him on his way out. You are very close, and coming here was a positive step. We will wait for you, for we are patient. When you see more of God's sins, you will become stronger in your convictions. When the time is right, you will return here and your body will be glorified. This is my will."

With that, Oliver's interview was over. He bowed once and walked away, leaving space for the next recruit to come in and present himself under Lucifer's gaze.

This time, Lucifer's smile was just a little bit wider.

CHAPTER SEVEN:

A COUNCIL OF WAR

The new recruits that joined his camp certainly helped, for almost immediately, Lucifer started winning more and more battles. It was never anything major, but they always seemed to show up at the right time to catch small groups of angels unawares. Azazel continued making more and more swords, but Lucifer's forces were focusing in on those, capturing weapons almost as fast as Azazel could make them.

By most estimates, Lucifer now had upwards of thirty thousand angels following his every order. The numbers and details of the host were sketchy, as they never congregated in one place for long. His mobile camp had been replaced by a series of seven camps, with several thousand hate-filled demons in each.

The loyalists had taken to congregating together as well. The rule of ten was abandoned for the rule of a hundred and this in turn became the unspoken rule of a thousand. To walk outside in a small group meant near certain annihilation.

It was that time when fear became a normal emotion for them. Some angels feared for Heaven, and some just feared for themselves. Alizel didn't know if some even started fearing for God Himself. To be perfectly honest, he wouldn't have been all that surprised.

The Father just sat there on His throne, almost as if the whole affair was meaningless to Him. Alizel really didn't see how His neglect was going to help anything. But, as Alizel reminded himself, God's ways weren't their ways. They knew it, but it didn't help some from getting so frustrated that they defected to the other side.

The tone of their conversations started to change, too. The phrase "It is complete and utter madness to oppose God" began to be heard less and less, although most still thought it. Subtle questions now worked their way in, some beginning to wonder if Lucifer did have a legitimate plan after all. As their numbers grew their status and legitimacy grew in turn.

Whether or not they feared, everyone was worried. They knew that without God's help, it was up to them to prepare. They couldn't rely on God to just say a word and return things to normal. Some said God wouldn't intervene, and some were even bold enough to suggest that He couldn't, but to Alizel all that talk seemed pointless. The end result was the same: they would have to prepare themselves.

A special meeting of the Angelarch was called to discuss just what they could do. Some were of the opinion that there wasn't anything to be done, though they still came to the meeting, mostly just to be in a well-defended place. Once the meeting got underway, however, it was clear that there were a number of things that they could do to be ready.

Michael addressed the greeting first. Though everyone else may have, Alizel was certain Michael never doubted the Father. He was so strong, so capable. Just seeing the poise with which he addressed everyone gave Alizel another sliver of resolve.

"Well met, my friends," he said, turning to look at the assembly. "Although the times are dire, the loss of others has helped us to realize the value of the friends we have left." He paused, running a hand through his black hair solemnly, and then continued. "We have come here to discuss our strategy and preparations for Lucifer's coming onslaught. Make no mistake. He will not rest until he is sent into the Containment."

A muted murmur passed through the crowd. Most had already guessed that Lucifer wouldn't back down until he had waged a massive war, but hearing it spoken from someone 'in the know' like Michael just made it all the more inevitable.

Azazel rose then. "Michael is correct, but the numbers, both of angels and swords, still favor us. With proper preparation, we will easily be able to defeat Lucifer's armies."

"What do you propose, sir?" Uriel cried out, the first time he had ever spoken at an Angelarch. Alizel guessed his Principality was one of the most anxious about the oncoming assault.

"There are several things that will help us," Azazel continued almost as if he did not hear the outcry. "The first, absolutely critical one is that anyone who has so far refused to train in the use of a sword must do so without delay. You still may learn enough to be of use in the coming battle." The way he said it was as if he blamed the angels who had decided not to train originally. Alizel looked around to see if he could spot Eleleth. If anyone had a right to say "I told you so" it was her. If the swords had never been invented, then none of this mess would ever have happened. But Eleleth was not there. Since the day Katel's troop had visited, Alizel had not seen her again. He couldn't bear to. He heard that as the war become fiercer she had continued to waste away a little more each day.

"I will be setting my lieutenant Verchiel in charge of training the new recruits." Verchiel was another who wore a sword at all times. He wore his slung over his shoulder instead of at his side as most angels did. The blade hung vertically down between the stumps of his golden wings.

Azazel's voice hardened suddenly. "We are also looking into developing a new weapon. However, for obvious reasons, I cannot discuss specifics here. Suffice it to say that the swords are very limited in range. We are looking at ways to project our power through a distance."

The audience murmured and shifted in their seats, perturbed.

"Are you sure this is wise?" The brown-winged Principality called Oliver objected. "Look at what happened the last time we tried to invent a new weapon!"

"Not only is it wise," Azazel countered, "it is necessary. I can assure you that Lucifer is tinkering and designing his own new weapons. Will we stand idly by while he grows stronger? Or will we do what it takes to strengthen ourselves? There is not one angel here who can deescalate this situation. Lucifer has made his choice. Now we must make ours. We must grow stronger, or perish."

There was scattered discussion among the multitudes, but it was clear that the majority felt that inventing new weapons was worth it. It was better to trade immediate safety for future potential danger.

Raphael rose. He waited politely for Azazel to acknowledge him with a nod before taking the floor. He spoke, his voice calm and his rhythm even. "There is another way that we can defend ourselves. It may not be much and we may not have enough time to make it for everyone, but God in His wisdom has offered us a gift of holy protection."

Alizel straightened up and sat on the edge of his seat, curious. Everyone hung on Raphael's every word with eager anticipation.

"Since the beginning, the Seraphim and Powers have worn metal breastplates, without really knowing their purpose. We have taken these for granted, just as we wear our albs or our colored sashes. By itself, this armor offers no protection. A Heaven's Blade can cleave straight through it in an instant. However, I have wondered what would happen if God's essence were used to strengthen our armor just as It strengthens the swords. I have asked the Father directly, and He has given us this gift. Thus, we can make protectors for our bodies, arms, and legs. With the infusion of the Father's essence, it will protect us against blows from the swords."

A loud cheer went up. This was fantastic news! Angels who hadn't smiled in quite some time broke out in grins from ear to ear. Of course, the angels all knew that having such armor wouldn't ensure their survival, but it would certainly give them an advantage in the fighting. And anything that meant less loss of life was a welcome sign. News like this had been a long time in coming.

"Of course," Raphael continued, "it will take some time to make this armor on a large scale. We are very fortunate, however, that the armor does not take nearly as much skill or time as the swords do. We do not need an atomic edge, only basic craftsmanship to ensure that the armor does not hinder our movement and flight. I should note that it is also possible to make large heavy suits that could theoretically cover an angel completely. We have investigated and decided against this possibility. For one thing, it would take a disproportionate amount of resources to make these full suits. It would be especially difficult to encase the wings in them. For another thing, such a suit might actually hinder more than help. If an angel's reflexes were slowed, then an unarmored and mobile adversary would be able to strike with their sword in one of the joints. Remember, all it takes is a whisper scratch from a Heaven's Blade."

He sat down as Alizel pondered this new development. It was obvious that Raphael had gone to great lengths recently to conceive of and design this new armor. Alizel was grateful that they had him on their side…but he was saddened by the responsibilities that Raphael was obviously taking on. This was the Seraph who had always been vying for peace, the gentlest of the highest rank. And now, he had to think like a military leader, like Azazel. It grieved him.

With Azazel on offense and Raphael on defense though, Alizel reasoned, it seemed impossible that Lucifer could triumph, no matter what his plan was. Yet, Alizel had to catch himself. He didn't know exactly how powerful Lucifer's troops had become, and what horrible weapons he had invented.

Michael rose and Raphael nodded to him. "This is welcome news, indeed. I am glad to hear of so much progress on this critical matter. Now, we turn to another defensive measure. To those that say it is impossible to construct something to keep out our flying adversaries, I now offer this. Orifel and his Thrones have already started an excavation project deep within Mt. Zion itself."

A gasp went up from the Angelarch. Alizel had certainly heard of no such thing! He didn't even know that such a thing was possible. As Michael explained it, he could immediately start to see the benefits.

"Many of our adversaries still have the ability to fly. Walls will not stop them. However, we are planning to build a series of tunnels. The system is complex, and the full map is known only to a few. Even those who are helping to excavate it are allowed to work only on one small area. We will create a maze of tunnels and certain key angels who need protection will reside there. Our command structure for the coming war can also be encased safely in the center."

It was brilliant. But something he said caught Alizel. He wondered who the "key angels" were. They were probably those like Eleleth who were too sick or unable to defend themselves. It did make a lot of sense to keep the command structure there, that way they would always be assured of receiving and sending orders and not worrying about spies intercepting their messages. He just hoped that they would be able to stay in contact with them while they were out on the battlefield.

Alizel himself hadn't really thought so much about fighting, but he knew he would have to eventually. He had trained with swords from the beginning; he wasn't one of the best, but he wasn't too shabby either. The memory of the times he had spent with Katel burned through his mind and a hot tear sprung to his eye. He had lost too much already. Lucifer was not going to take anything else.

"If it comes to it, the caverns will also be where we make our last stand," Michael continued.

The leader of the Cherubim suddenly rose. Ophaniel rarely spoke, but when he did everyone paid extra attention. Although Lucifer mostly drew his support from the Unranked and other lower orders, he had received defections from every order of angels. Every order except the Cherubim, that is. Not one of those closest to God had betrayed Him and gone over to Lucifer's side. They remained at their post, always and with unwavering loyalty, no matter the doubt swirling in the minds of all the other orders. The highest ranking defect Lucifer had received was a Throne named Malphas.

All four of Ophaniel's faces were now something that could only be described as human children. His youthful appearance belied his wisdom. Alizel had always wondered why those closest to God appeared in the simplistic guise of a child.

"The Cherubim will make our last stand at the foot of the throne of God," Ophaniel said quietly, and with an unobtrusive sense of authority. "I do not think our adversary will try a direct assault, but if he does, we will gladly hold next to our Lord."

The Cherubim were a numerically small and militarily insignificant order. They were too close to God's ways. If God himself fought, Alizel was sure that they would jump into the battle with pure-hearted joy, but as it was, God was still silent. Perhaps He was waiting for the precise minute to turn the battle. Or, perhaps the battle and result didn't matter to Him. Perhaps He just wanted to see what everyone would do. It was all very perplexing.

Michael nodded. Alizel couldn't tell if he was troubled at being interrupted, but if he was he soon forgot it. "The last preparation that we need to make," Michael began his conclusion, "is to learn to fight as a unit. There are individuals here who are very skilled with the blade, no doubt. However, if we all learn to fight together, we may protect each other's weak points. This will give us the advantage we need. Remember, an individual confrontation, even an entire battle, can be turned by a very small margin."

It was necessary, Alizel realized. He hadn't considered the value of tactics before, but they had in fact been using primitive ones all along, since the first battle in the Angelarch. Things like forming a half-sphere, guards flying forward ahead of those they wanted to protect…all of this made a big difference in the battles. Looking at the importance of formations and strategy now, he wondered what else he had overlooked.

"The training in formation and battle tactics will be undertaken by Verchiel, who is an intelligent strategist and teacher. Everyone who is not otherwise employed should attend to his practice whenever he has free time. The training will be done in the first opening of the caverns. It is large enough for practice and we may keep away from Lucifer's prying eyes there." Michael turned to recognize Verchiel.

Verchiel always had a way with words. When he spoke, it filled those who heard with a longing to go out and be great. He stroked his red goatee thoughtfully before he addressed the crowd.

"The days when we took carefree strolls through the garden of the Lord are over," he said grimly. His usual smile was gone now. "The days when we played and laughed and danced are over. The days when we explored the Universe to learn its mysteries are over. The days when we will fight for our very existence are coming. We must be ready. We will be ready!" His eyes burned with clean fury as he spoke. He said nothing else, and returned to his seat.

Michael regained the floor, solemn. "We have made great progress today, my comrades. We have a new armor that will protect us, new training to undertake, development of a potential new weapon, and construction of a safe haven inside of Mt. Zion. Much work remains to be done. We do not know how much time we have until our adversary begins his assault. This meeting is hereby adjourned. Let each angel go to the task prepared for him."

Walking out of the Angelarch, the buzz was louder than it had been for quite some time. That meeting had done much for Alizel's morale, and by the words and gestures of those around him, he could tell that he wasn't the only one who felt a newfound sense of hope. The worst part about sitting around waiting for Lucifer to pick them off one by one was the feeling of helplessness, the idea not only that they couldn't stop it, that they didn't even know how to stop it. Now that they had a specific plan with several concrete steps, everything appeared brighter.

Alizel wouldn't have said that the angels thought their leadership was abandoning them, it was just that some thought they should have come up with a plan earlier. Now it was clear that they had been contemplating what to do all along, and had some cunning ideas to implement. *What else have they thought of?* Alizel wondered. And what had Lucifer thought of? One thing was for sure: the coming battle would be of such epic proportions that it that would be remembered and retold for eternity.

"That armor idea is brilliant," Mupiel came over beside him, a huge smile across his face. "It seems so simple. I wonder why none of us thought of something like that before."

"Maybe someone did," Alizel offered, "but just to be safe, only told Raphael about it."

"That's a good thought," he conceded. "That's the last thing we'd want Lucifer to know about. Although, I'm sure he still has some spies in our camp. It's just too bad that we can't spy on him, since he makes everyone in his camp use hate."

"It is a disadvantage," Alizel agreed. "But knowing about the armor won't do him much good. It's not like he can make it himself, since he needs to infuse it with the Power of God. Plus, I'm not even sure if he'd be able to wear it. If he is so against God, I wonder what would happen if he tried to put it on."

"Well, in any event, I feel much better now than I did before the meeting. We have so much we need to get done, and no idea how much time we have. We need to get started right away!" Mupiel was energized and ready to go.

Alizel felt the same way himself. Lucifer's attack could come any minute, or it could come in months or years. One thing was certain, though. The more prepared they were, the better. There wasn't a minute to lose.

"Well then," Alizel smiled, "I guess you and I are off to the caverns."

They weren't the first angels to make it into the caverns. A hundred or so were already milling about, admiring the new defenses. The antechamber where they first entered was rather large, allowing several hundred angels to congregate comfortably. The walls were smooth and dusty brown colored, with several veins of darker materials running through them. The echo of Alizel's sandaled feet was lost amongst the excited whispering.

He glanced around quickly, but didn't see Verchiel anywhere. There was a line of angels leading toward something, however. He signaled to Mupiel and they both went over to wait in the line.

"I haven't been this excited for a long time," the angel in front of him was saying to another. "This place is amazing. I'd like to see Lucifer try to get in here!"

"Excuse me," Alizel said, tapping him on the shoulder. "Is this where we are to practice our tactics?"

The angel just smiled. His name was Hyveriel, and although Alizel wouldn't say that he knew him well, he had certainly spoken with him many times before. Although there were nearly one hundred fifty thousand angels, they had been in Heaven for over fifteen billion years. That's a hundred thousand years for each angel— and they never forgot anything. Of course, they spent most of their time with those angels who were closest to them, and barely ever talked with the higher ups, but Heaven was the most close-knit community imaginable. He supposed that's why the war was so painful.

"No, Alizel," Hyveriel said, grinning. His skin was the color of honey and his feathers were sapphire blue. "This is merely the registration line. We must all give our names and abilities, and then they will divide us into squads and battalions later."

"I was wondering how we would be organized," Mupiel cut in. "Originally, we could have used our groups under our Archangels and Principalities, but we've lost so many to the Containment and Lucifer since then that our former structure seems to have no merit for war."

"I'm only telling you what I've heard," Hyveriel cautioned, "but it does seem necessary. However, the defenses of this place are such that even a few can defeat many."

"How do they work?" Mupiel asked, glancing around as if he could see the hidden defense systems.

"I don't claim to know," Hyveriel answered. "All I've heard is that there are many connected rooms throughout the mountain. They're joined by long, thin tunnels that burrow through the rock. Each individual will have to fly though in single file. That way, no matter how many Lucifer brings against us, we can't be overwhelmed by numbers. The tunnels have small slits in their walls, space enough for only a Heaven's Blade. We can wait on the other side and just cut them to pieces before they enter."

Alizel immediately saw the brilliance of the plan. The tunnels could branch off several times and many would just lead to dead ends and certain ambush. A full frontal assault of Mt. Zion by Lucifer was doomed to fail, as long as Michael's forces could convince the demons to follow them in.

They soon made it to the front of the line where an angel named Numinel sat recording information in a long scroll. His iridescent-feathered pen scratched along the parchment as a many-colored script burst forth from the tip. His own feathers bore the same rainbow hue as his pen. Angel feathers made the best quill pens known, although few angels would suffer to give up a feather for something considered so superfluous. Records were usually unnecessary, since angels had perfect memories, but sometimes writing something down gave it more power. It also put things in a slightly different way. For reorganizing the army, it could be a big help.

Mupiel and Alizel gave their names, experience with a sword, rank and position within the hierarchy, and other details. Numinel was very thorough (which helped to explain why the line was so long), asking questions such as how fast they could fly and which hand they wielded the sword with. Alizel guessed somehow the higher ups would use all this information to design an optimal organization for their forces.

After passing through the table, they had to wait again for an escort. When they had a group of eight angels together, a stern faced angel came to bring them to the main training center.

"Follow me," he said brusquely, "and stay close. No one is allowed in the tunnels without supervision. That's to make sure the map doesn't get back to Lucifer, as well as for your own safety. If you get separated, stay where you are and call for help. Otherwise, you'll be hopelessly lost." He was obviously impressed with the authority of his job.

"I doubt it's 'hopeless,'" Mupiel whispered. "We could always fly around at full speed until we've tried all the possibilities and we're bound to find the right location sooner or later."

"It would be later," the escort said, "much later, if at all. Even without angels actively defending them, the caverns have a myriad of traps. Walls shift, rocks fall, and well…other things you can't know about. Other things even I, who helped construct them, cannot know about. In fact, I only know the way to the meeting place. So without further delay, let us head there now."

Mupiel and Alizel just glanced at each other. What kinds of things were hidden away inside these rock walls?

Their escort threw out a knotted line of rope and told them each to grab hold of it so that they would not become separated. Alizel was last in line, and upon entering the narrow opening, immediately felt claustrophobic. Angels were meant to soar majestically, not barely flutter their wings to float by. It helped somewhat to alternate bursts on the wings so that they spiraled through. In any event, the going was not very fast.

The pathway had been lined with a luminous moss that cast an eerie glow over the whole affair. The rock was dry and gritty, and the glow was just faint enough for Alizel to make out the basic textures of the sides. As they passed by, he saw several possible defense openings. Small slits seemed perfect for thrusting a Heaven's Blade right down at an adversary who would be powerless to stop it. The angle was such that the blades from the defenders would come in perpendicularly, while the tunnel was not deep enough for an attacking demon to raise his sword at such an angle. A knife would work, but only a few had ever been made. Such a weapon would only be effective against an unarmed angel, for angelic swordplay was a game of speed and tactics. However, even if someone did manage to get a knife through, it wouldn't be long enough to hit the angel on the other side.

Alizel didn't know how long they twisted and turned, but soon he realized that even with his perfect memory, the shifting route would make it difficult to find his way back. He felt the coarse fibers of the knotted rope dig into his fingers as he grasped it tighter. This was his only lifeline.

Only once did they pass another group of angels going the other way. Alizel wondered how the caverns could accommodate two groups passing each other, but there were small branches built in where one group could wait while the other group passed. As he flew through and waved to the other group, Alizel realized how effective the branches would be for hiding an ambush.

He was quite relieved when they finally arrived at their destination. They made it to a larger area that could only be the practice field. The area was much bigger than the original entrance cavern and his feeling of enclosure lessened somewhat by gazing at the high, vaulted ceilings. The rock face was still rough, and it appeared that the angels building it hadn't wasted time with niceties. Small groups of angels were flying all around, sparring with thin metal rods.

They landed in the middle and bid their guide farewell. "I hope you enjoyed your brief tour of the catacombs," he said, a glint of pride in his eye. "You are to report to Verchiel over there," he stopped to indicate the far corner of the open space, "while I take back a group who has already finished. Good luck. Formation training is important, but after traveling through our fortress, well, I think we all know what is going to win this war."

He was sincere in wishing them luck, but Alizel could also tell that he believed very strongly in the fortress he had helped to make. Why shouldn't he? From what Alizel had seen so far, his pride was justified.

They made their way over to Verchiel, who was assembling angels into groups of sixty-four for training. Alizel's group was the second to last group of eight to arrive, so they only needed to wait a few minutes for one more group to get started. When they were ready, they sat down while Verchiel addressed them.

"Welcome to formation and tactical training, my friends. Here we will teach you ways to protect each other in combat, and how to break through the formations that Lucifer is likely to use against us."

Verchiel spoke loudly, confidently. Hearing him further calmed Alizel's fear of being in an enclosed space.

"Many of you already know how to use a sword. This is of the utmost importance. If you do not use it well, you will fall. When you do, you will create a weakness in the formation, and put the rest in danger. If one stands, all stand."

Certain Powers came through the group and started passing out crude metal swords. Alizel had used a Heaven's Blade a number of times, and he immediately saw that there was really no comparison. The swords were nothing but a long metal cylinder crossed with a shorter one right above the handle. A true Heaven's Blade was light, balanced, and fit snugly in the hand. It could be commanded with the speed of thought.

"These are your practice swords," Verchiel continued. "You will use these until you demonstrate proficiency with them. Formations are useless if the individuals in them are weak. If one stands, all stand. Do you understand?"

"Yes, sir!" They replied in unison. "If one stands, all stand!"

They spent the next several hours in small groups practicing basic sword fighting techniques. They went over cuts from every direction, stabs, blocks for each of the cuts, evasive flapping of the wings, and what to do from the position where both swords were locked together on the inside. It took a while for Verchiel to be satisfied, but soon even those who had never held a sword before were picking it up. After the basics were complete, they started working on more advanced techniques. They chained together blocks and strikes in powerful combinations, worked on spins and flips to evade an enemy or get to a good position on them, and spent a good deal of time on fakes and deceptive movements to trap an enemy into starting an attack where he would put himself into a vulnerable position.

Alizel already knew most of the techniques and tricks from his sparring matches with Zebub, Katel, and Uriel, but it was always good to have a comprehensive review and work with other angels. The last part of the individual combat drill was sparring. Although it certainly wasn't the same as facing an opponent with a real live blade, it was still very helpful to work with a number of different partners. They did a bit of one on one and two on one sparring, and then broke into groups of eight where one would stand in the middle and the others would stand around him and attack him from all directions.

Once Alizel got past the terror of seeing a number of angels attacking him at once, the drill was actually fun. He had to admit that he recoiled in shock the first few times that he was touched with a blade. Even though he knew the training swords couldn't hurt him, his memories of the ambush that led to Katel being sent to the Containment made him jumpy. His perfect memory could relive every battle, every strike, every scream as the essence of an angel was sent away. He would never forget them.

After they had rotated and given each angel a chance in the center, Verchiel called a halt to the proceedings and had everyone gather again.

"Excellent work, my warriors." Although Verchiel's underlings gave compliments freely, Alizel thought it was the first time he heard the Power himself give one to anyone from his group. "Your skills are passable, but you must take every opportunity to hone them further. Have no illusions—those in Lucifer's camp are doing so at this very hour."

Alizel hadn't thought of that before, but it made perfect sense. Of course Lucifer and his army would be practicing. He had a majority of the angels that had practiced with swords from the beginning. Their training had already been going on for several days, but as they needed no rest, they were ready for more.

"Now, it is time to train in groups." Verchiel didn't waste any time as he continued. He was business-like, efficient. With tens of thousands of angels to train, he could afford to be nothing less.

"Watching the seven on one sparring, I saw all of the groups naturally go into a particular formation. Can anyone tell me what that was?"

One of the angels in a group opposite Alizel raised his hand and spoke. "It was a half-sphere, sir. We surrounded the target on foot while a couple attacked him from above."

"Yes, that is exactly correct. Yet, I did not direct any of you to make a half-sphere. Why did you do it, then?"

The angel thought for a moment and then responded. "I suppose it just made sense because that was the way we could all get at a piece of him to strike."

Verchiel nodded, seeming satisfied. "Precisely. The half-sphere is a critical formation for combat. This is the best way to attack an individual. At the same time, it is also the best way to protect an individual or an object. Just as the half-sphere attack pattern makes use of the greatest number of vulnerabilities, the half-sphere defense formation reduces the greatest number of vulnerabilities. The other reason that I made you do the seven on one drill was so you would get the idea of what it feels like to face foes on all sides. This is a feeling I hope you never have to face in combat. If we do the half-sphere correctly, then none of us will have to face an enemy coming at us from more than one direction. If one stands…"

"All stand!" the group shouted together.

It was brilliant, and simple. With one drill, Verchiel had not only told the angels what to do, but also let them teach it to themselves. They spent the next several hours practicing all manner of half-sphere drills, forming them of different sizes with different groups of eight. The most common formation and the one that would likely be used in battle was a half-sphere that consisted of twenty-four angels on the perimeter and eight on the inside of the half-sphere. Some were standing and some were hovering. The eight on the inside were to serve as backup in case one of the angels on the outside fell. Thus, they were assured that the other forces would not break the formation if only a few angels fell. This formation was to be used on the ground, with all of the angels on the shell facing outwards.

After the half-sphere they worked on the full sphere. The full sphere was just a natural extension of the half-sphere, but for when they were airborne. The leader of the sphere was the angel on the inside who would look out and manage the fight on all sides. It was his job to make sure that each point of the sphere was reinforced as efficiently as possible.

They covered many other variations, such as when they were backed into a corner. This was actually an advantage, since it gave less surface area to defend. They kept drilling over and over, Verchiel's subordinates flying around the spheres and trying to trick them by sending phantom enemies from each side, and darting in and out to strike with the metal blades. Alizel's group's job was to practice shifting angels around to reinforce the sphere where the fighting was heaviest. It took a few hours to get it right, but soon Alizel's confidence started rising.

This might actually work.

After the exhaustive lesson on formations, they went into different scenario drills. Angels acting as enemies came at them unawares, and they had to form up spheres of different sizes depending on the circumstances. They always tried to make one big sphere, but sometimes they would be cut off from their companions and forced to make two smaller ones. When those fell, they were forced to fight with their friends back to back.

"Halt!" Verchiel called out when he had seen enough. He had a slightly satisfied grin on his face, but his eyes still betrayed his anticipation of the dangers ahead. "We have made significant progress. You will now return to your quarters so that the next group can be brought in. You will return here for one week every seventh week, until…well, until you receive orders otherwise. In the meantime, you must practice."

"What should we practice, sir?" Mupiel asked from beside Alizel.

"I have saved this piece of information for last," Verchiel spoke slowly, looking each angel in the eye in turn. 'Because it is one of the few pieces of information that we know about hate. Crossing swords with an angel is the best way I know to tell if someone is playing you false. After training with you lot, I believe that you will all be true to God. What we have seen so far of the enemy is that although hate can make them nearly as strong as God's Energy, it also tends to make them reckless. Spend no more than ten percent of your time focusing on offensive skills. Spend the majority on blocking and countering, and faking. Remember, due to the lethality of the Heaven's Blade and the speed at which even those filled with hate may strike, the angel who bides his time and evades and counterattacks simultaneously will have the better chance of winning. Spend most of your time on this."

With these last few words a different angel came to get them. They spread their hands once again on the knotted rope, and were soon back at the entrance.

The return journey had been a blur. Alizel was nearly lost in thought thinking of what horrors were awaiting them on the day that Lucifer finally decided to strike.

That day didn't come the next day or the day after that. Things continued to be much the same in Heaven. For his part, Alizel wasn't sure if this was really a positive development at all. If he didn't catch himself, sometimes he wondered if the waiting wasn't worse than an actual battle. It was nearly killing him on the inside to sit and do nothing, knowing that at any minute Lucifer's armies could strike. However bad the waiting was, though, he knew that the actual fighting was going to be worse. Much worse.

At least they had not squandered the time. He had made three more visits to the caverns to train, and the armor production was in full swing. Alizel had even received a set of silver arm guards and a matching breastplate. Azazel had really outdone himself on the swords, and most of the army had them now.

Putting on the armor calmed him. It wasn't that it offered foolproof protection. Without a full set, Alizel would be lucky if it deflected even a glancing blow. It was more the feeling of putting the armor on. The protectors covered his body with a warm glow, the essence of the Father, and It was comforting to have It so compacted and close. Although he felt Him around at all times, it was a thin, mist-like feeling, nothing like approaching Him or feeling His essence infused into the armor. The first time he put it on, Alizel couldn't help but shudder with the thought of what it felt like to be touched with a sword, again remembering the fear shooting through his being during the ambush that had nearly claimed his own life along with Katel's. He had only heard screams from angels sent into the Containment, but whether the screams were from the sensation of the blade itself or from the agony of transitioning into another state of existence, he neither knew nor cared to find out.

He was training in the gardens by himself when it finally happened.

The gardens of Heaven had deteriorated during the rebellion. Angels no longer could afford to casually stroll down the paths, listening to trees gently swaying and gazing into streams of shimmering crystal. There were too many spots open for ambush, too many ways to separate an angel from his companions and attack him before he knew what was happening. The flowers, which previously had displayed beauty untold, bursting forth in brilliant shades and hues that no human eye would ever behold, were now dull and listless, seeming to reflect the moods of those around them. The unbridled joy of years past was truly no more than a memory.

Alizel heard a movement behind him in the brush and spun with the speed of thought. He let out a sigh of relief when he saw that it was only Uriel, but his relief evaporated as quickly as it had arisen upon seeing his grim visage.

"I've been looking all over for you." His voice and body were tense. "We need to report to Mt. Zion and form up immediately."

Alizel swallowed, but did his best to stand straighter. "Yes, sir!" He did not have to guess why they were being summoned. It was time for war.

CHAPTER EIGHT:

A BATTLE JOINED

The foot of Mt. Zion was swarming with troops, most forming up in companies of one hundred twenty eight, the best number to form a sphere. Some spheres were made from as little as eight angels, but most were of the larger variety. A smaller sphere had the advantage of being faster and more mobile, but a larger sphere offered more protection. Still, the larger the sphere, the more chance the enemy had of breaking through.

A group of eight angels was called a patrol, while four patrols worked together to make a squadron. Four squadrons made a larger sphere, which was called a company. Ten companies went together to form a battalion, and included the battalion commanders and the messengers needed for communication between the battalion's various companies. The battalion's commanders were connected to the main strategic leaders of the army through messenger angels that were darting back and forth, organized under Gabriel himself.

As Mupiel had suspected, the entire host had been reorganized after the mass loss of angels to the Containment and Lucifer's side. Everyone still had their rank from before, and members of the higher orders were peppered throughout the army in various positions of command. The Seraphim were generally at the top, while other angels headed up various divisions and companies.

Uriel was the head of Alizel's company of one hundred twenty-eight angels. From the looks of it, they were the last two to make it back.

What a time to have left the protection of the group! Alizel hadn't been gone that long, but after staying in groups due to constant fear of attack, he had wanted just a few moments of solitude to focus his thoughts and dwell on the past. It was difficult sometimes for him to keep a clear head amidst all the tension and anxiety of the past few months.

"We've detected that Lucifer has sent out a small force," Uriel was filling everyone in. "We're not sure what the purpose of the advance guard is, but our battalion has been chosen to fly out and meet them."

"Sir," Hyveriel asked, "why must we fly out to meet them? Can we not draw them into the caverns?"

"Those are not our orders," Uriel responded, a grim look on his face. Alizel hated seeing the toll the responsibility of military command had already taken on his dear friend. "We must meet them in open battle first to see their tactics. We will fall back to Mt. Zion only when absolutely necessary."

There was a general mumbling in the group, and Alizel could tell the others didn't like this idea any more than he did. None were looking forward to facing Lucifer's hate fueled minions on the battlefield.

"The High Command has assured me," Uriel continued, carefully choosing his words, "that everything we do will be of immense strategic value, and that the Lord would never sacrifice any of you needlessly."

Alizel suddenly appreciated the difficulty of Uriel's position. He wanted to do everything he could to reassure them, but couldn't risk giving out too much information that he had received from above. That is, if those above him had even told him enough to be able to reassure his troops. Alizel was sure that they were keeping their plans very close indeed.

"Everyone is ordered to check and recheck your equipment, and then that of your neighbor. Make sure your swords are at the ready, your armor fastened, and formation positions double-checked."

Uriel's instructions were largely unnecessary, as they had already set about their preparations. Alizel had taken to wearing his forearm protectors and breastplate nearly all the time. They were currently strapped tight. He refastened his breastplate anyway and looked around at everyone else. They were ready as well. They were fortunate that everyone in their group had swords. Though Azazel's efforts at sword-making had successfully armed nearly every angel in the army, they had still run out of time; some angels in other groups would have to wait on the interior of their spheres until they could procure swords from their companions who had fallen or captured weapons from their enemies. Alizel wondered how many swords Lucifer's side would have, and how those without them would attempt to fight.

It was only a few minutes before the order to form up came. Alizel was stationed on the bottom edge of the full sphere, which was, relatively speaking, a good place to be. His entire squad formed the bottom part while on the ground. When airborne, Alizel and his squadron would still be closest to the ground while the rest of the sphere hovered above his squadron. Once aloft, the entire sphere could move in any direction, so if they dropped down on an enemy, Alizel's squadron would be leading the charge.

"Listen up, company." Uriel's admonition was unnecessary as they were all now looking at him with rapt attention. He pointed to Alizel's squadron first. "You will form the bottom of the sphere. We will start the battle in Defensive Formation Alpha, meaning you will start on the ground in a half-sphere, ready to reinforce the other three companies above as gaps form in the sphere above or on your flanks. You will listen for my order, upon which we will change to Offensive Formation Gamma, where you will provide reverse cover to sphere as it moves." He gave similar instructions to the company's other squadrons.

The angels around Alizel nodded. Although their entire battalion was in the most danger of any of them, Alizel's squadron was the safest in the company. Still, without knowing Lucifer's plan and if they could counter it, none of them were really safe. No one would be, until they destroyed the menace once and for all.

Alizel was grateful that Raphael was the commander of his battalion, and all eyes were on him as he stood in conversation with a messenger angel. He nodded once, then took a deep breath, staring at the horizon. He raised his arm, strong and straight to point in the direction of the enemy. His soft brown wings now flared and his platinum sash with its crimson "S" bunched up on his shoulder as he did so. His message was clear.

With one voice, the angels sent up a mighty cry, and flew to meet their foe.

The angelic host paused once they had sighted them, a teeming black mass just visible on the horizon. They were coming straight toward them, and each company quickly set up their half-spheres on the ground. Angels stood or hovered, depending on their position. They had only to wait.

If the other side wanted a fight, they would attack the reinforced half-spheres, and it would be easy for the angels to defend. However, if the demons attempted to fly above the line of defense on the ground, the loyalists would have to rise up and use the full spheres. A half-sphere on the ground was better for defense because they had to defend less than half of the surface area of a full sphere. It would be interesting to see what kind of formation Lucifer or his generals used.

The two armies were near the middle of a vast plain that stretched for many thousands of meters. The lush grasses had not yet dried up, and the cool blades calmed Alizel as they poked between his sandaled feet. The companies set up their half-spheres in two rows of five, with enough space for a demon to fly in between each. If anyone did, they could be attacked from both sides.

Although the formation was great for defense, the enemy could easily fly around on the sides and flank or pass by them if they preferred not to engage. In that case, some half-spheres would have to break off and pursue with attacking patterns instead. Alizel dreaded this outcome. It would mean a loss of even more angels to the Containment, and give the other side a much higher chance of winning the battle.

Soon they came into view, and Alizel cringed at the sight of them. Although he had seen many hate-fueled angels before, they were often hidden behind trees or in small groups. Now, there were five or six hundred of them all together, crying out in hideous voices. It seemed that they had morphed into new forms as well, although most still resembled the angels they had once been. Their wings had lost all feathers and were thick and leathery. Alizel noticed with relief that many of them seemed not to be able to fly. Their useless wings were folded and atrophied on their backs.

His relief quickly faded, though, to see that most of them indeed had swords. Many had other weapons as well, items that Alizel could only guess the purpose of clutched tightly in their muscular fists. Some had long poles, crossed with other staves at various angles—pitchforks, sickles, and other weapons.

As the enemy stared them down, Alizel didn't see in them any of the fear or anxiety that he felt in his own heart. They were stomping their feet and pounding the butts of their weapons on the ground, all with a ceaseless bellowing and screeching. It was the most horrifying sound he had ever heard, even worse than the screams of dying angels.

One who still had the ability of flight hovered above the rest and paused for a brief moment, glaring at the lines of loyalists in front of his horde. Suddenly without warning, he thrust his weapon up in the air and screamed out with a screech that somehow rose above the din of his followers.

His message could not have been clearer. As one, the enemy rushed forward, heedless of tactics or strategy.

"Form up and hold!" Uriel shouted out his order. "They're coming!"

Alizel was surprised to see them charge forward almost as if they had no leader. In a matter of seconds, they had closed the gap and were upon Alizel's company.

His position on the inside of the half-sphere gave him an excellent vantage point on the battle around him. He would not have to engage until any of the angels in his battalion were destroyed and left a gap in the sphere. Then he would have to rush up and fill it before any demons went through.

As Verchiel had predicted, Lucifer's minions were not patient fighters. They did not wait and try to draw out an attack. They just slammed themselves against the half-spheres, which shuddered but held. The strategy of waiting for a counter-attack worked well, as the demons tended to focus in on a single target only. While fighting against one angel, they were open to attacks from the side and rear. Alizel smiled as he thought of his training. Their training and formations were really making all the difference in the battle.

After a few minutes, Alizel could see that it was indeed possible they could win the day, with what he hoped would be only a small loss of life. Although the horror was all around him, he felt oddly detached since he had not yet swung his sword.

Unfortunately, he knew that the other side could see much of the same. They did have leaders of a sort, apparently, for one of them ordered a group of demons who were still able to fly to pass around the side of Alizel's company

Uriel saw the threat and reacted immediately. "Offensive Formation Gamma! Go!"

"Yes, sir!" They echoed and switched without hesitation. Alizel's squadron shifted to form the bottom of the sphere, launching upwards away from the main battle in order to pursue the rogue attackers. Alizel's hand tightened on the hilt of his drawn sword.

They shot right into the middle of the attackers, dividing them from their comrades. This group somehow managed to fly even on their ragged wings, although by the looks on their faces they were exerting great effort to stay aloft. One of them whipped around to face Alizel with a spiked ball attached to a stick. His wings didn't have the surface area of Alizel's and looked to be made of a heavier material. He had to flap them several more times for every one time Alizel flapped his.

The demon swung the stick, and Alizel raised his blade to parry. The sword blocked the staff but the ball swung around and smacked him in the arm.

He cried out. Pain was a very unusual sensation. Alizel felt it as if he were in a daze, his heart racing as he fluttered his wings several times to keep aloft. He focused his vision, concentrating until it narrowed around the demon.

Within a second his body had recovered, and he brought his sword down on the rebel. He blocked it with his staff, but Alizel switched it up in a flash and thrust it right into him. He screeched as he went to the Containment.

It was the first time he had ever sent a demon into the black place of Un-being. It unnerved Alizel, but he had to block it out of his mind and not think about it, the only thing that was going to save him from streaking into the Containment himself. He realized he had to be automatic, without remorse, dispatching judgment on every traitor to God that he saw. They would not hesitate to end Alizel's existence if they got the chance.

He faced another demon, this one with a sword. He came at Alizel straightaway, telegraphing his strike and not bothering to feint or hide his intent. Alizel brought his sword up to block. As they struggled in a solid lock, the blue-winged angel next to Alizel struck at the exposed attacker. He screamed as his soul was banished, and Hyveriel caught the enemy's blade as it fell.

"Better we have this than them," he said smugly, tucking the blade into his belt.

Alizel grinned in thanks and looked around for another attacker, but the few around him were all but gone.

He took a second to survey the battle raging below, hovering above the chaos. One of their half-spheres had been destroyed, but the other eight were still in defensive formation. Theirs was the only company that had switched to an attack sphere. Very few of Lucifer's attackers were still standing, and those that were now found themselves outnumbered and having to fend for themselves on all sides. It was over. Alizel was surprised at how quickly and completely they had won the battle.

In truth, it seemed far too easy.

However, now was not the time for gentle musings. The companies flew back down to their original formation, and Alizel settled to the ground. In a few minutes the order came to form up to Defensive Formation Beta, which was a ring around the battle site. One company went to the middle of the ring and scavenged all of the enemy weapons. They took everything, including the crude-shaped implements that Alizel was sure had almost no military value. It was laughable to think that the fallen angels faced off against a Heaven's Blade with a metal pitchfork, but those who had attacked had done so in all seriousness. Still, every clue about the enemy was potentially important, as they could help Azazel determine things about the other side's training and fighting abilities.

When they were finished cleaning up the field, orders came to reform their companies and retreat back to Mt. Zion. They had won a great victory that day, and all breathed an enormous sigh of relief. If the rest of the battles were anything like this one, Alizel figured, the war would be short and easily won indeed.

A great celebration ensued at the foot of Mt. Zion after the battle. Michael ordered that the entire army remain encamped for the duration of the conflict. No one had any illusions that what was won was anything more than a minor skirmish, but it certainly had been the largest battle so far. More than that, they had successfully used their formations and tactics for the first time. It wasn't so much that they had won, but how easily and swiftly they had done so.

Mupiel and Alizel were seated a little off to the left of the main encampment, and could hear the cymbals crashing as the entire host praised God and thanked Him for the victory.

Alizel reclined in a wicker wood chair that gently sloped backwards. Angelic chairs had wide bases but were thin in the middle so as to support the back without encumbering the wings. Mupiel could barely remain seated for more than a few seconds, as he kept jumping up to replay one confrontation or another.

"And then I blocked it on the inside, just like they taught us." He was up again, the hapless branch from a tree in his hand in lieu of his sword. "You should have seen his face, Alizel, I don't even know if he realized that I had him. Anyway, I switched the blade up, and then sent it straight to his neck."

Apparently not all of the others felt the guilt that Alizel did at destroying another angel, even one who had rejected God. On the one hand, he knew that it was their duty to destroy those who threatened Him. Although He had never given this explicit commandment, Alizel knew it to be the case. Otherwise, why would all of the angels and demons be engaged in the war? And, unless they fought them, the demons would take every chance they could to send the loyal angels into the Containment.

Still, something about it wasn't right. Even though the hate distorted the others' bodies and features, Alizel could still often remember the angel who was underneath. Was it really right to destroy them? Or was that what was best for them? Was the place of Un-being better for them than living with hate? Although the concept of partial sacrifice was foreign to angels, such a thing had been observed on Earth. An animal might chew off a part of its paw that was caught under a pile of rocks and live life with a little less of its body rather than die whole. Were the hate-filled angels the dead branches that they needed to prune for the tree of Heaven to grow higher? The idea was very disturbing.

"Mupiel," he said, interrupting his friend who continued swinging the tree branch around with reckless abandon. "Why do you think God does not heal the rebels?"

Mupiel stopped his hacking the air and responded confidently. "I have pondered that before. I think He can't heal them if they don't want to be healed."

"What do you mean God *can't* do it? You know He is omnipotent!"

"That is a tricky problem," Mupiel agreed. "And I've been asking around. The best answer I've come up with is that God chooses to limit His omnipotence by letting us exercise our own free will. Although I'm sure He *could* step in and force us to make any decision, that's not what He wants."

"I'm not sure I understand."

"Think of it this way. The only way that the rebels still exist now is by focusing all their energy on using hate. God's Energy still radiates through Heaven. All one of those angels would have to do is just will it in his heart to be reconciled to God. Then God's Energy would come in and their body would return to its former glory. I have heard of it happening a few times."

Alizel had heard of such a thing too, although it was exceedingly rare. "I guess that makes sense, but the problem with hate is that it distorts the angels' ability to reason and think logically. Some of them probably don't even know that the way of reconciliation is open to them if they should but wish it."

Mupiel shook his head slowly. "That is one of the tragedies of hate." His voice was suddenly sad. "Once an angel starts using it, it is very difficult to stop. It is an addiction, that way."

A thought suddenly occurred to Alizel. "What if another side effect of hate is fighting poorly? We certainly seemed to have an easy enough time with that battle."

"That's it!" Mupiel's blond hair bounced as he struck his fist into his hand. "That could explain why God Himself hasn't ended this whole thing! Maybe He is just letting us all sort it out ourselves. He must surely know all about hate and how it works. He must have known that this war will be easy for us to win, so He does not trouble Himself about it."

Alizel wasn't convinced, although the idea did have merit. "Perhaps it also gives more time for the angels who have turned away to repent." After he said it, he realized how much the two reasons together could explain God's behavior. Alizel had always known that God's ways were not their ways, but even so he always struggled to understand Him. His heart was full of praise and admiration for the Most High, and seeking to understand Him was a natural extension of this, however confusing He was at times.

He could see that Mupiel thought highly of his idea as well. "Alizel, you're brilliant!" he said, slapping him on the back. "He knows that our armies face no real danger in the field. And it's always been said that God is a longsuffering God. He wants the war to continue as long as necessary, because while the rebels are still alive, there is still a chance that they will come back."

The thought was almost perfect, except for one flaw. "But, what about us?" Alizel countered. "I mean, although God lets the conflict drag on, certain loyal angels are bound to be sent away into the Containment. What about them?"

Mupiel's face dropped. "That is a good point." He thought long and hard for a few moments. "Maybe after the war is over God will open up the Containment and let all the loyal angels out."

The conversation continued on like this for some time. The sinking in his stomach lessened somewhat, although Alizel didn't feel like they had really gotten to the essence of God's reason. He did feel like they might have figured some of it out, though; things made a bit more sense. Of course God would still love those in rebellion against Him. He would want to give them time to repent, but He couldn't force them to repent. God's omnipotence was total, save where it ran into the individual free will of each angel He had given him to use. God still possessed true omnipotence because His limited omnipotence was limited only by His own free choice.

It was quite baffling, but made sense, after a fashion.

Their hearts filled with joyous revelry as they rejoined the main camp. Stories of the battle, cheers of hope for the future, and praises to the Most High God burst forth into the air for the next several hours.

They didn't have long to savor their victory. Lucifer's forces were spotted converging on the field in front of Mt Zion the next morning and they went out to meet them with renewed confidence. This time, it seemed like the majority of his troops were there. At least, Alizel hoped it was the majority of his troops.

In the distance, he thought he could make out what used to be his friend Verin, as well as a few others that he knew, though it was difficult to be sure. His heart sank.

The horde arrayed against the loyalists was immense. Seeing so many fallen ones all gathered together like that sent a chill down to the middle of Alizel's soul. It looked like nearly one third of the entire host, close to fifty thousand souls, was striding forward. They carried all manner of weapons, and took all manner of forms. Alizel looked hard at how the hate had affected each one differently. Although each angel had always had a distinct appearance since creation, they all looked similar, and were certainly recognizable as belonging to the same species, the same creation. Now, some of the enemies were short and squat, some tall and thin, and some all manner of contorted shapes in between.

What really got to Alizel, though, were the faces. Although all parts of their bodies had changed, the rebels' faces were where he noticed the biggest difference. Their eyes were distorted, hollow and vacant, yet filled with simmering malice. The skin of their faces had been stretched in some areas and bunched in others, subservient to the changing facial structure below. Were not his brave brothers in arms standing shoulder to shoulder and wing to wing, Alizel was not sure whether he would not have fled headlong out of fright.

This time Michael needed to bring out the entire army to face them. The fact that they had nearly two times as many fighters as Lucifer, and that they had already proved the effectiveness of their formations gave Alizel little comfort on seeing the vastness of their enemy. It wasn't so much that he feared for his own self, but his heart sank with the realization that there would be hundreds, or even thousands, of angels who would be going into the Containment within the next several hours. He felt like jumping up and crying for everyone to stop, to cease this madness, but he knew that his cry would be as useless as Eleleth's had been. Nothing short of direct intervention from the Father could stop this conflict.

Lucifer's army came forward, and Michael set up their defensive half-spheres again. This time Alizel's entire company was in the rear, so they were free to watch the first part of the fight, held in reserve to replace those companies on the front if they were destroyed. Although they had griped about their assignment the day before, by facing the horde first in a small skirmish, they had received a safer place on the day of the major battle.

The angels on the front lines quickly set up their half-spheres in rows of ten. While setting up full front-facing lines would have been better when meeting a ground-based enemy, there were enough of Lucifer's minions that still had the power of flight to justify using the half-spheres.

Lucifer's army came forward to within about one hundred paces from the first row of spheres. Alizel was certain that they would not have to wait long, but as he watched, something started worrying him.

The monsters facing them wanted to fight. That much was certain. What were they waiting for? In this type of battle, the attackers were at a distinct disadvantage. Would they hold their lines and force the angels to attack? Would the commanders give the order? The discipline of this force was markedly different from what they had faced earlier. Michael's lines held steady, stern-faced angels reflecting the glory of God, while the other line started taunting. From the back, Alizel couldn't make out their exact words, their voices all blending together in a menacing, deafening screech.

Fortunately, the loyalists were not forced to endure this for too much longer. The rebel lines parted and Zebub suddenly emerged from the breech. His appearance was even more loathsome than before. His body had become bloated but the edges were rotting. Alizel could see several angels in the front lines cover their noses to avoid the stench. For a brief moment he felt a twinge of curiosity over the myriad effects of hate on their adversaries. It almost looked like Zebub's body was generating new material in his core as fast as the outside was rotting and falling off dead. They had no microorganisms in Heaven as they did on Earth, so Alizel did not know how this was possible.

Zebub began addressing the host, and Alizel's curiosity turned once more to revulsion at the demon's figure and words. He could not believe the filth that Zebub spewed forth. Alizel had heard that Lucifer had changed Zebub's name even as he had changed his own, but even in his mind, Alizel refused to refer to anyone but God as "lord."

"Lord Lucifer has assembled a show of force to appeal to the reason of every angel here as well as the Lord God Himself," Zebub's voice rose as both armies fell silent. "Our Lord Lucifer is merciful. He would feign not destroy the beauty of Heaven. He is willing to accept your surrender under the following non-negotiable conditions."

Alizel didn't see how Lucifer was in any position to start demanding anything. He was the one in rebellion. He was the one who needed to surrender in order to avoid being destroyed!

"The first condition is that every one of you bow down and acknowledge Lucifer as supreme ruler of the Realm of Spirit and the Realm of Matter. You must also acknowledge myself, Baal Zebub, as his deputy. The second is that the Lord God may keep His place as Creator, but must acknowledge His error in placing man before angels."

Cries of disbelief and "Blasphemy!" erupted from the army. This was too much! How could they expect the army of God to follow their demands? Had hate really disrupted their thoughts to the point where any of them believed this insanity? Alizel was almost beside himself with rage.

"For the third demand," Zebub continued, raising his voice again to speak over the din, "God must apologize to all angels, and bow down and thank Lord Lucifer for chastising Him. The final demand..."

But they never did get to hear what the final demand was.

The front line of loyalists surged forward almost before anyone knew what was happening. All the years of insecurity, the pain of losing loved ones, and the anxiety of the war burst forth from the angels in a holy fury that enveloped them. The demons were an affront to God by their very existence. The demand that God bow down to Lucifer was just too much. Lines broke, formations dissolved, and even the commanders themselves were caught up in the initial rush. Alizel even saw Michael rush forward ahead of the rest, leaving a trail of vanished demons in his wake.

The demons already had their weapons raised, and began swinging left and right in tight lines as soon as the angels came at them. In that instant Alizel saw their trap. How could they have been so stupid to charge?

Yet, how could they have the patience to sit there and let them blaspheme like that?

These demons were both better armed and better trained than the ones they had faced before. It was obvious from the beginning: they protected themselves from the sides and rear, and the physical differences between each one gave the angels some trouble. The loyalists were trained to fight in a highly effective but standard way. The myriads of demonic shapes gave them all sorts of advantages. An angel might be engaged with one who had kept his normal height while a taller one brought his sword slicing down from above or a shorter one would run through the angel's legs underneath and catch him with an upward thrust to the stomach.

After a few horrible minutes of battle, the screams of their compatriots had a sobering effect on the loyalist troops. After the initial flare of energy, most on the front lines had seen the trap that they had been led into. The command was trying to reestablish itself, calling for retreat back to their original lines.

But forming up now would use valuable time, since the spheres on the front lines would be unable to form in their original groupings due to the heavy losses they had taken. This battle was nothing like the one before. It was turning out all wrong!

A platinum blur jumped forward, Azazel assuming command. Fortunately, he had not gotten caught up in the initial rush. "First group fall to the rear! Second line, change to Defensive Formation Alpha. Other formations shift forward one!"

Lines shifted as angels hurried to their new spots. The reinforced half-spheres sprung up almost instantaneously to halt the sea of red and black that was threatening to drown them.

Fighting was fierce on the lines. Alizel felt fortunate to have his vantage point where he was far enough away to not be in immediate danger, but close enough to witness every slice, block, and chop. It was only out of curiosity that he wanted to see what was happening. He didn't allow himself to think too long on the actions of the individuals fighting. He knew that he couldn't, and still retain his sanity. Thinking about what the demons were was bad enough; seeing them try to destroy those angels who he had lived with, played with, and praised God with was almost more than he could handle.

Lucifer must have given a command to the demons, as the back part of his force split into two and tried to flank the angels on both sides. Michael, back at his post, responded and sent out two companies to each side to bring out lines at forty-five degrees to their main line. Alizel's company got sent to the right side. This time, he was on the outside of the sphere, facing directly towards the oncoming attackers.

They did not hesitate to come with everything that they had.

For a split second he didn't know who to attack as several targets came at him. He unconsciously inched backwards, seeking out an extra sliver of safety from his companions. He felt his wings brush back against the sleek softness of those standing next to him, and it gave him the extra ounce of courage that he needed.

Several limbs swung at him at once, it seemed. In the mass of misshapen demons that surged at them, it was hard to tell which leg, arm, tentacle, or snout belonged to which adversary.

He was in pure defensive mode, content to block and parry everything that came at him. He dared not lunge forward to take an obvious opening, as doing so would not only open him up, but leave the angels to his sides defenseless as well. *If one stands, all stand*, he reminded himself over and over.

Whenever he could strike the enemy without reaching too far, he took a shot. A poke here, a slice there, and he could start to untangle the mess that was facing them.

Just as the lines of enemies were becoming clearer to Alizel, a huge winged beast leaped overhead. He actually had Heaven's Blades anchored to the claws of his scaly feet.

"We've got it!" yelled two of the angels hovering near the top of the sphere. To defeat this enemy would be extremely valuable, as they could capture the blades he had attached to his claws.

The beast cried out with a screech so horrid that it rent the din of the battle. It stabbed its claws straight at the attackers, but as they parried the thrusts, the other blades attached to its claws by ropes swung around and sliced the angels. The beast's forward movement was enough to swing the blades to take out anyone who was facing it while they were attempting to block the first strikes. By the precise timing that this required, Alizel knew this beast had been practicing.

He saw several angels jump forward from the middle of the sphere to reinforce where their partners had been lost. A few more flew up as well, to counter the beast from the top.

A beast with six eyes and six horns charged forward to face Alizel, and he had to turn his attention away from the flying threat and face this one. His attacker only had a short dagger, but this time Alizel did not have to be very patient. He skewered the demon before he could get within striking distance.

Alizel couldn't say how long the battle wore on before Lucifer's side finally called a retreat. Well, strictly speaking, he *could* have said as angels did have perfect memories…but he refused to look back on that horrid time in any great detail. Whether it was a day, week, or month, the battle raged fiercely with neither side giving the slightest bit of quarter. This was the real enemy, ruthless, strategic, and powerful. As angels still in communion with God, they had been prone to discount the power of hate, especially when they had seen it only in small doses.

But there was no discounting it now. When thousands upon thousands of infected angels all charged together…certainly they had seen the real strength of the enemy.

The army regrouped back at the foot of Mt. Zion. They had lost over a quarter of their troops. How many the enemy had lost was not certain, but Alizel estimated about one third to one half. It was little comfort. How could anyone look at a life, and rejoice that *only* tens of thousands of irreplaceable souls had been forever lost in a single battle? The fact that God could choose to open up the Containment as Mupiel suggested was little solace.

As he brooded over this in his mind, Alizel came very close to finally doubting God. He wasn't proud to admit it, but the whole thing seemed such a waste. And although He might preserve a victory for those who were left, what of those who had fallen? Where was their victory?

There had to be some higher purpose to the war. That is, if God was omnipotent. Well, if God was both omnipotent and beneficial. Alizel didn't want to admit the possibility that God didn't have complete control over the situation. Yes, it might explain things better if he thought that it was possible for God to lose control. He could still be the strongest, wisest being in existence, but that didn't mean that He had *complete* control.

There was no doubt about it, no way to get around the issue. Bad things were happening. It was as simple as that. Bad things were happening to good, loyal angels. Of course God did things that the angels could never understand. But this…

Neither option was tenable. Either God was not in control, or He was in control and was purposefully letting bad things happen. Alizel just didn't know what to make of it. What was the point of this entire war?

Alizel had to push the thoughts from his head. He just couldn't handle it anymore. Maybe when this whole thing was over, there would be some answers. He didn't think God Himself would come down and fill them in like He had over the creation of man. But, at least it would be nice if some of the higher-ups could explain some of the main questions.

They didn't have much time to rest. They didn't need it, and it was clear that hate was a more or less steady source of fuel for Lucifer's troops. Michael made some small adjustments in their formations, but there wasn't time for large scale retraining, for the next day, Lucifer's forces came again.

Alizel didn't know whether the losses had affected them psychologically or not, but they did seem to attack with a new determination. This time the battle was fought at the very base of Mt. Zion itself. Alizel never could have imagined that it would come to this, but here they were. The mountain itself was too massive for Lucifer's troops to surround, and Michael's forces spread their half-spheres out over less than a quarter of it. The spheres bubbled up against the mountain, using the slope as a part of the sphere they didn't have to defend. They reinforced the ends of their main lines instead, in case Lucifer tried to outflank them.

Alizel couldn't imagine what Lucifer's plan was. After all this, it was finally time for him to show his hand. Alizel's company was lined up directly between Lucifer's forces and God. He glanced backwards over his shoulder to see God's Glory burning from the Throne. The Cherubim still ringed the Lord, facing inward. They did not seem to mind the trouble below.

His eyebrows furrowed in perturbed curiosity. Were the flames of God's Energy blazing just a bit differently?

Did God feel sorrow at the choices they had made?

He turned back to the front, his doubt and confusion swirling through his mind. Had Lucifer's forces come to Mt. Zion to attack God, or had they chosen to attack Michael's army and come to Mt. Zion simply because that's where they were camped? Alizel had seen many things that he didn't believe, but he still couldn't imagine that Lucifer would march right up and try to…what? Slay? Threaten? Blackmail? God? What could Lucifer do? What! Lucifer's own weapon came from God himself. Could Lucifer stand there before the majesty and power of God? Lucifer could not even stand in God's presence without His permission.

Still, Lucifer knew the inevitability of this truth as much as Alizel did. Had hate really destroyed his reason so much?

Yet, searching back, Alizel remembered the time when Lucifer and Gabriel had been talking during the beginning of Zebub's rebellion. Lucifer had mentioned the existence of a plan *before* he had rejected God. One thing was sure—Lucifer's endgame was near.

They were methodical as they attacked this time. It was times like these when the armor really proved its worth.

It was entirely possible for the angelic host to defeat the horde on the field of battle. Somehow, though, Alizel had always considered the clash of armies to be of only secondary importance. It wasn't that the higher orders, even the Seraphim like Lucifer, Michael, or Gabriel, could outfight an entire army. They had prodigious skill, to be sure, but their value was more as a commander, a strategist, or a rallying point. Still, in the back of Alizel's mind, he had always figured that tide of the battle must be turned with a clash of Seraphim. But what if things worked out differently? What if God's army, using armor, numerical advantages, superior tactics, and the inherent weakness of hate, simply triumphed on the battlefield? Though many angels would be lost, the victory would be no less complete.

The fight wore on and on. The relative thickness of the lines kept only a small fraction of either army engaged at any one time. Lucifer's troops were skilled and patient. These ones would neglect to take a potentially fatal strike if they knew it would leave them open. It was not uncommon for a single confrontation to persist for fifteen or twenty minutes. Yet, the armor was of great worth. A demon might penetrate the defenses of an angel only to be frustrated by the armor he wore underneath. Nothing that the demons possessed had even the faintest chance of slowing down a Heaven's Blade. Once one of Alizel's comrades made it past the other's sword, each hit landed true.

The depletion of their forces from the previous battles had had one beneficial effect. They had taken the armor from those who had been lost and now nearly everyone had armor on. Alizel had picked up a helmet, and most of the angels at the front end of the sphere had breastplates and shields as well.

The battle was going well. The enemy was again losing more troops than the loyalists were, and Alizel wondered how long Lucifer could afford to keep it up. Still, the angelic losses were painful.

Thus, he was surprised, but only mildly, when the retreat order came. Although they were winning, Michael ordered everyone to fall back to the caverns inside of Mt. Zion. Alizel didn't have to ask why. The caverns were impenetrable. Let Lucifer and his followers try to come in there! Although it would take more time to defeat them, they would be able to manage it with far fewer casualties.

Falling back took some time, with the army forming up several spheres over the various entrance tunnels to Mt. Zion. They gradually shrunk the sizes of the spheres as angels entered the stronghold. The last ones through had a bit of a time, but the majority of the demons did not follow them. The screams of the first few that did gave the horde pause.

As he looked around at the angels still alive inside the cavern, Alizel felt a great sense of relief. So many were gone into Un-being, but so many still remained. Alizel didn't have much time to ponder, however, as soon a commander came by and ordered them to move away from the entrance, to safety farther up and further in.

CHAPTER NINE:

LUCIFER'S ENDGAME

Lucifer surveyed the scene around him. His camp was set up on the outskirts of the battle. It would be a lie to say that the mood was mutinous. Yet, there were many grumblings. The war had taken a turn for the worse once they had been forced into the catacombs. They had started the entire campaign at a two to one numerical disadvantage, and through the lost battles had whittled their numbers down to roughly a four to one disadvantage by the time of the last major battle before the angels had retreated to Mt. Zion.

The fighting inside Mt. Zion was worse yet. It was extremely frustrating to have to enter single-file, and be slaughtered by an unseen enemy. So far the demons had sent several hundred troops to the protected fortress, and none of them had come back alive. They had no idea if their patrols were dead or just hopelessly lost. It also seemed unlikely that they had even been able to take any angels into the Containment with them.

"These cowards will continue to hide and pick us off one by one!" Abbadon spat. "They should face us on the open battlefield."

"Although that's what we all wish," Kasadya countered, stroking his black goatee as if his mind was somewhere else, "it would be foolish of them to do so. With the walls as well as their armor, they make a trap that it is dangerous for us to enter."

"Well, we have to do something!" Verin smashed his fist into his other hand. "We can't just wait around for them."

"We must be patient." Kasadya shrugged. "We need to stick to the plan."

"The plan? The plan?" Verin chortled, his red hair aflame. "What has the plan done for us so far? I mean no disrespect," he caught himself, "but the time we goaded them into attacking us first was about the only good thing we did."

"One thing is for certain," Baal Zebub complained, "we cannot win the battle like this. We've lost most of our army. They have a great defensive advantage. As I see it, it's hopeless for us. Let's face it. We've lost, through *his* bungled command! I should have remained your leader. There's no way we can win this battle!"

His statement was out there. Although the look on his face showed that he might have wished to take it back, he couldn't. Everyone turned to look at Lucifer to see how he would deal with this problem.

Lucifer sat on his throne, only half listening. He was, if anything, amused by the panic in his counsel. He looked around at each one, his gaze lingering just long enough to make each uncomfortable. He gave half a chuckle.

"Win the battle? Why would I care about that?"

The shock of his remark cut through the council. Even the usually imperturbable Kasadya looked confused. "My lord?"

Lucifer shrugged. "Honestly, it doesn't matter if we win or not."

The demons were aghast. He could see they feared that he might have finally lost his mind.

"My lord!" Oliver exclaimed, momentarily sickened. "Are you saying that this whole war has been for nothing?"

"Certainly not. The war has served its purpose very well."

"Its purpose?" Oliver's incredulity was reflected among the demons. They all had the same thought. Why had Lucifer not told them his real plan?

"I hope you don't think me stupid enough to challenge God outright with a war." Lucifer's face showed that he was not really surprised. "How could I expect to win that way?"

The demons hung on Lucifer's every word.

"No...we cannot defeat God openly. But, we can destroy Heaven and escape while it falls around His being. We will go to a new location that I have prepared for us, and our sovereignty will be supreme there."

If any of the demons had grasped Lucifer's plan it wasn't apparent by the looks on their faces.

"My lord," Abbadon questioned, "how can we hope to destroy Heaven?"

Lucifer smiled, relishing his impending triumph. "It's quite simple. Every order of angels has a specific task associated with it. Yet some of the tasks are known only to the order that holds them...and to me. One of those tasks is that which is entrusted to the Thrones." He paused. "The Thrones actually hold up Heaven in their bodies."

It took a while for the gathered counselors to take his meaning, but once they understood, smiles spread over their faces.

"You can see how I could not risk telling anyone of the plan," Lucifer continued, expounding. "It required all of the pieces being in place before my masterstroke is ordered."

"My lord!" Abbadon exclaimed. "There is truly a reason you are the Bright One! But, surely Michael knows of this threat."

"Undoubtedly," Lucifer agreed.

"That means the Thrones have to be hidden deep inside Mt. Zion."

"Oh, they are," Lucifer agreed again.

"And probably guarded heavily, by some of the fiercest angels," Abbadon pressed.

"By Azazel and his crack Powers, indeed." Lucifer nodded.

He could see that his demons were once again stumped, wondering if perhaps he was about to announce that this was a joke or that he really had lost his mind.

Lucifer just laughed once more at the bewilderment of his generals. "My friends, do not think you are the only ones loyal to me." He paused for effect. "Azazel has seen the light of his own reason since almost the beginning.

"More than anything," the Bright One continued, "Azazel loves weapons. He knew that staying with God as a spy for us was the only way that he would be able to direct things to ensure that thousands of weapons were created and brought to use. In the battle, the borders have been neglected. I have already prepared our place." Lucifer raised his hand. "The final victory awaits only my signal."

With that Lucifer walked over to a large ceremonial brazier. He extended out his hand slowly, folding in his little finger first and then the rest of the fingers in turn like a fan being closed. He clenched his fist tighter, energy surging throughout his powerful arm from the shoulder down. With the suddenness of a snake strike, he opened his hand, shooting a ball of fire into the brazier. Burning on nothing, the fire caught and shot straight upwards, the great signal of Lucifer visible over all of Heaven.

The demons gave a cry of triumph, and turned to face towards the battlefield.

"Yes," Lucifer exclaimed, panting from excitement, "you shall rejoin the battle. Rejoin with the knowledge that our victory is sealed. When Heaven starts to fall, return to the Portal where we can go to our new place. The Portal does not just lead to the Realm of Matter. It also leads to other places in the Realm of Spirit."

The demons pounded their weapons on the floor in excitement. This type of hope hadn't existed since the beginning of their rebellion.

"There's just one more thing," Lucifer spoke quietly, and the rest immediately fell silent. "You," he said, pointing to one of them already at the edge of the throng. "Oliver, is it? Come here."

"Yes, sir," Oliver answered, coming close to Lucifer. He was out of place in the herd of demons, the only one who had still kept his angelic appearance.

"You have served me well as my spy," Lucifer said. "You have given us much valuable information. Now, you no longer need to take fuel from God. Indeed, His presence here in you is offensive to me."

"My lord!" Oliver exclaimed. "You know I exist only to serve you. But let me go now as I am for one last attack. The Thrones will not suspect me."

"Do you think you can succeed if Azazel were to fail? No, he will not fail me."

"Well then," Oliver continued, "let me stay as a spy for you here in Heaven. Please forgive me for presuming to offer you but a humble suggestion. I could come to your new location and pass you information."

A fleeting shadow crossed Lucifer's face. "Once we leave, if Heaven still survives, there will be a chasm fitted across it so wide that none can pass across." He drew his sword and pointed it at Oliver. "Either you are with us now and forever, or I will destroy you myself."

He was waiting in the shadow of a tree, his breathing quick and shallow. The jet of fire still burned upwards from Lucifer's camp. Of all the things it might mean, none of them were good. Gabriel folded his grey wings back and scanned the horizon again.

There was still no sign of him.

Demons were covering everything, trying vainly to breach the sides of the mountain he was on. Gabriel furrowed his brow in worry. *He should have been here by now.*

He glanced back at God Almighty, and thought he saw His glory blazing even more brightly, but it was hard to tell. Even for one of the Seraphim, it was impossible to look upon the Father too closely without hurting his eyes.

He looked back at the tree again. The branches were healthy, but the leaves had started to show a malaise on the ends. Although it was far better than other parts of Heaven, Gabriel was saddened to see that the poison had reached even here.

He grimaced. He could not afford to wait much longer.

At a noise on his left Gabriel turned, and the demon he saw made him draw his sword. Yet, this demon was unlike the others. It was hesitant, and stumbling, still getting used to its body.

"Gabriel!" it called out. "I am here."

Gabriel looked at the demon more closely. "Oliver!" he gasped. "What has happened to you?"

"Lord Lucifer is a great master, but a hard one," Oliver spoke slowly, filling Gabriel's heart with a heavy sadness. "He has turned me to this once he set his plan in motion."

"The plan! Oliver, you must tell us. What does he intend to do?"

"Tell you? Why should I tell you anything? You're the one who did this to me!"

"Oliver, listen carefully to me," Gabriel grabbed Oliver by the shoulders. "The hate has lowered your ability to reason. But you must still accept God and come back to us. It's not too late!"

"It's too late for me, my friend." Oliver's words had almost a mocking tone to them. "I've seen too much." He clutched his head with both hands and cried out. "It's too much! I can't control myself!"

"Oliver, there is always a choice with God. It is never too late for Him!" Gabriel cast about franticly for a way to save his friend. Could he grab him and drag him bodily towards the Father? How could he extract Lucifer's plan from Oliver when he was like this?

"You have done enough to 'help' me already!" Oliver shouted, writhing in his new body.

"Then help me too!" Gabriel pleaded. "Tell me what Lucifer would do."

Gabriel looked into Oliver's eyes, and saw something he had never seen in any other hate-filled angel. Oliver was fighting. He was fighting against what was happening to him. But did he still have enough reason left?

"He..." Oliver stammered. "He plans to destroy the Thrones. Azazel has turned. Lucifer has prepared a new location and he will take us there."

Gabriel's mind was racing. Azazel turned? He certainly had had suspicions for some time. But, he was the one guarding the Thrones!

"Oliver, we have not a moment to lose! Come with me to the Father!" Although time was critical, Gabriel couldn't bear to see Oliver like this, especially when it was on Gabriel's account that Oliver had volunteered to be a double agent in the first place.

"No, no, I cannot face Him like this!" Oliver wailed. "It is too late for me!" He ran backwards, drawing a sword and brandishing it in Gabriel's face.

Gabriel grimaced with pain. He knew he could overcome Oliver, but to do so would probably render the information Oliver and others had sacrificed themselves for useless. With one last backward glance, Gabriel turned from Oliver and dove into a tunnel in the mountainside.

When he woke from his sleep he saw that the sun was already nearing its zenith. Its rays spilled down his face, and Adam realized that he was hungry. He had to go but a few paces before he saw a succulent fruit hanging down from a tree, and he plucked it and took a large bite straightaway.

It seemed so long ago that God had mentioned cultivation of the soil. Adam himself had no idea what that could mean. He did not set a hand to the plow nor tend to the fields. There was such abundance in the garden that he never had to go more than a few steps to find a fresh meal. Each bite held such flavor and nutrition that he felt satisfied and refreshed in only a few minutes. Food was never a concern for him.

Adam looked to the sky with a frown. For some reason, he felt the slightest twinge of apprehension. He saw the clear blue of the day and the twinkling stars of night. He had never really wondered what the stars were, those things were best left to Eve. However, today felt different.

Eve came over then, a look of worry on her face. Adam surveyed his bride. "You feel it too then?"

"As if the world were ready to be torn asunder," Eve answered. "What could be happening?"

"God would not forsake us now," Adam replied, trying to sound more confident than he was. "What did He tell us? Eat everything but the fruit of those two trees in the center of the Garden?"

"That's right," Eve nodded. "The Tree of Life and the Tree of Knowledge of Good and Evil. You haven't eaten of them, have you, my love?"

"No," Adam replied. "I have eaten of many trees, often not knowing the nature of their fruits before I eat them. But I know those trees. If you even walk near them, you feel…different. I don't know what to call it, but they're not the same as the rest of the trees. I don't think that we could eat from those trees by accident."

"You're right," Eve agreed. "Still…I don't know what I feel today. There is a great sadness in the air."

She slid closer to Adam and he draped his arm around her, drawing her in. "It will be okay, my love. We must trust in God and He will take care of us."

Eve nodded and relaxed a bit, resting her head on Adam's bare chest. She stared off into the distance. What would the future bring for them both?

Alizel paced through the corridors. He had gotten to know the labyrinth much better since they had been driven back into the caverns, but he still knew only a small portion of the tunnels. There were roughly a dozen larger rooms, each big enough to comfortably hold about a tenth of the remaining troops. They were all encamped there, if it could be called that, spending much of their time simply waiting. The pace of the war had slowed considerably during the last few days. Alizel couldn't imagine any large battles happening inside. The space was just too confined.

The word that he had heard from those closer to the surface was that the demons were still trying to infiltrate, but were suffering heavy losses and not making much, if any, headway. As far as Alizel knew, nothing more than a few surface tunnels had been breached, and those had been quickly retaken by their own forces. It appeared that their plan was working well.

He had to admit that although he was grateful they had stemmed the loss of life on their side, he would be glad when they were back out in the open air again. The Energy of God did permeate the mountain—it was His mountain, after all. They were still able to feel fully powered and energized. Yet, Alizel longed for the outside, for the Heaven that was before the conflict.

Alizel wondered how long it could last like this. They were at something of a stalemate. Lucifer's armies had learned that they couldn't hope to take the caverns. Any attempt brought massive losses and little progress. Yet, Michael's forces did not want to stay here forever either. They could launch a surprise attack, perhaps even attacking from many places at once. But though they would almost certainly win, they would suffer bitterly in the end. Someone still had to face Lucifer in combat.

"Come here, Alizel."

Alizel jumped at the voice, startled. Eligos, one of Azazel's Powers, came up to him and bowed. "I need to head over to chamber six. Would you mind accompanying me?" They had a rule that angels were never allowed out and about by themselves.

"Certainly, sir," Alizel replied. He wasn't doing anything else, and he was happy to help a Power. Usually the Powers kept to themselves, and it would almost always be two of them traveling through the tunnels together. Eligos's request struck Alizel as odd, so he glanced around. None of the other Powers were there to be seen, and this relieved his suspicions. Eligos simply didn't want to wait for another of his comrades.

They passed the tunnel sentries with just so much as a nod from the gruff guards.

They didn't talk much as Eligos led the way. Alizel trusted him to lead, for he traveled the tunnels with the quiet confidence of one who had traveled the same path many times.

All at once, the mountain shook with a terrible tremor like none Alizel had ever felt. He reached out his hand to steady himself against the rough wall of the tunnel. What was that? Had Lucifer unleashed some new weapon that had the power of shaking Heaven itself?

Eligos seemed to know more about the earthquake, but all he said was "We have to hurry!" When Alizel questioned him about it, he mumbled some unintelligible reply, and pushed forward ever faster.

It didn't take long before they reached their destination. It was not chamber six. They were in a side tunnel quite off the beaten path that opened up into a small room. Crossed swords barred entry to anyone. Eligos calmly strode to the two Powers who were securing the room and spoke an entry password. The swords parted and Alizel stepped into the room as well.

Inside Alizel saw two more angels besides the ones guarding the door. Seated at the far side of the room was Bodiel, his former teacher and one of the twelve Thrones. Next to him was another Power, standing with his sword drawn. His face had a tense sadness to it.

"Now."

Eligos spoke his simple word, and the whole room erupted in confusion. The armed Power stabbed his sword straight into the body of the Throne without a moment's hesitation. Bodiel didn't even have time to scream before his body was sucked into the Containment.

Immediately, Alizel felt another tremor identical to the first. There was no doubt about it. With a sickening sensation in the pit of his stomach, he knew Bodiel wasn't the first Throne who had fallen.

The jarring impact shook the room, and the assassin pitched about. The two Powers guarding the door lost no time setting on him and sending him and Eligos into the Containment. A second after everything had started, it was all over, ending with the Powers pointing their swords at Alizel's neck.

"I had no idea, I swear loyalty to God alone!" Alizel was frantic, hoping that they wouldn't just decide to destroy him rather than take any chances. "I don't know what's happening, but we have to protect the others!"

Alizel's last point seemed to convince them.

"Give me your sword, and follow us," one of them said. "If you are truly loyal to God you will have it back."

He didn't want to hand it over, but he wasn't about to argue with these two, especially not when the rest of the Thrones were in danger. Alizel gave the handle to the nearest one and the Power sped off into the corridor.

Alizel followed him without a second thought, the other Power just behind him. It seemed like a kind of madness to be going straight into trouble, but he had no choice, not if he wanted to help save the rest of the Thrones. He couldn't believe that wise, gentle Bodiel was gone! All he could keep thinking about as he rushed down the corridor was his teacher's lesson about the boulder crashing into the pond below, how small actions could change the course of the future.

They hadn't gone far before they felt another tremor. This one rocked Heaven so hard that they had to hold up and wait for it to subside before they continued on. Alizel was getting worried. If these tremors got much stronger, they could reconfigure the paths of the tunnels in Mt. Zion, leaving them hopelessly lost, or trapped. Even worse, the whole mountain could cave in. Was that Lucifer's plan all along? Alizel couldn't imagine God allowing that to happen. True, he never thought that He would have let things get this far. But a collapse in the mountain could affect the throne of God Himself!

Boulders were falling in their path every few feet, and the Powers had to blast them apart with powerful blows from their speeding fists.

Soon they were at another opening, and Alizel had a horrible feeling as he saw the swords of the guards scattered on the ground. The three of them leapt in and saw that the target was still alive.

Orifel, the greatest teacher and head of the Thrones, stood weaponless and defenseless in the corner of the room.

Towering over him, with sword drawn and weapon lust in his eyes, was Azazel himself.

Oliver raced down the mountain, not daring to look back. How could they have done this to him? He had risked more than anyone. The others had stayed safely behind their lines and their armor, waiting for the information that only he could give. And yet, what was behind the way Gabriel had looked at him...was it loathing in his gaze? Contempt?

A part of Oliver told him that it had been nothing more than pity, or sadness even, that had marred Gabriel's visage when Oliver went to give his final report. The strange feeling stormed up within him and pushed these thoughts away. What right did Gabriel have to pity him? They had always thought themselves better than everyone, those Seraphim. They gathered in secret, dreaming up plans of how to run everything.

And those plans had consequences. Good angels had been sent straight to the Containment, and for what? Just so Michael and Gabriel could get Oliver close to Lucifer.

The part of him that was fighting for his sanity reminded him that those angels had volunteered to sacrifice themselves, and that it was bravery to sacrifice oneself for the greater good.

But was the good really good?

Was an army that asked its members to destroy themselves worth fighting for? Was it right to be a part of such a force? His mind conveniently pushed aside the fact that Lucifer had done much worse—he had created a war for no other purpose than for a diversion.

Was there anyone left who was blameless? Any who could stand before the Father with alb as white as the day of their creation? Oliver felt the fiery love of God emanating from behind him, and he longed to turn back into it. Yet, how could he face God now? Could God forgive and welcome him back? Did he even want to go back? In his heart he did, but in his mind, he wondered. Being around Lucifer for so long had clouded his judgment.

Talking to Lucifer was an unsettling experience. Every statement he said made sense, every argument sounded perfectly benign and logical. There was always something underneath, in the heart, that one knew what he was saying couldn't be right. Yet, it was never easy to say exactly how he was wrong.

He felt the intensity of the Father's energy change, increasing and yet at the same time becoming mellower and even…sorrowful. It was the feeling Oliver had every time one of the angels was infused with hate, but magnified thousands of times.

He had already used it. Could he now go back? Did he want to go back?

With torment in his heart and without any particular destination, Oliver staggered down the mountain.

"Don't do it, Azazel." Orifel's voice was calm and composed. "Think about where this will lead you!"

"Enough talking, doomed one." Azazel did not flinch in the least. His silver eyes narrowed. "There is no way around it. To destroy Heaven, you must die!"

At the last word he brought his sword down with all his might. They were all powerless to stop him. Alizel's scream of terror died in his throat as he braced for Heaven to come crashing down on him.

He heard only a loud clang.

Looking up, he saw Orifel's forearm raised above him as he crouched in defense. Alizel's heart leapt. Orifel was a large, odd-shaped angel. Under his robes, he must be wearing armor!

That's not all that was under his robes.

Orifel shoved Azazel back and stood. His features seemed to suddenly melt, his long cloak falling from his shoulders and slipping to the ground. His extra eyes fell too, leaving another angel emerging from his disguise.

It wasn't Orifel at all.

It was Raphael.

The Seraph stood there, golden armor blazing with the Light of God. His bearing was tall and noble, firm and stern. His previous gentle nature, the nature that had begged for peace and fought for any means of staving off the war, was gone, and in its place was a warrior ready for battle. Looking at him like that, Alizel knew that there was no one else to face Azazel. Only then did Alizel realize that Azazel had shed his armor and sash, and was now standing there wearing only his alb.

The shock on Azazel's face quickly turned to mirth, even joy. "Well, this is truly a fortunate development. I thought to simply destroy a weakling Throne, and yet I shall have sport with one of the mighty Seraphim first." It was hard to tell if Azazel was afraid. If so, then the mocking undertones were his way of showing it.

Raphael shrugged, unimpressed. "Orifel has been hidden where you will not find him. But that does not matter. Today, the day when you first face the Armies of God, will be the day when you first taste defeat."

Azazel brought the hilt of his sword up to his heart and swept it downwards in the traditional salute. "Then let your actions prove the truth of your words!"

Raphael kept his sword in his sheath, but nodded in return of Azazel's salute. "As you asked, so shall the truth of your wretched state be proved upon your very soul."

Azazel didn't wait for Raphael to draw, but lunged forward in a rage to strike from above. Raphael stepped into the blow, and caught Azazel's wrist before his sword could fall. They grappled for a split second before Azazel brought both his feet up and kicked Raphael backwards.

Raphael staggered and Azazel advanced, sword weaving in front of him. He struck several blows, but Raphael blocked them with an opposite pattern with his forearm gauntlets, negating Azazel's efforts.

Azazel jabbed his sword forward sharply, and Raphael dodged to the side, bringing his forearm guard smashing into Azazel's face. The head of the Powers cried out sharply in pain. It was a new sensation for him, and by the look on his face, extremely unpleasant.

He roared in rage and launched another attack, missing only by a razor thin margin.

Raphael had not yet drawn his sword, and now Alizel was beginning to wonder if he had any intention of doing so. He seemed to be fighting a very dangerous game against the Power. While Alizel was impressed that Raphael had survived so far, surely he couldn't keep this up forever. Was he waiting for something? That couldn't be it, because the three angels who were still in the room, himself included, would have gladly rushed in. Was he toying with Azazel? Or did he really wish not to destroy him?

But how long could he really expect to keep up against the onslaught he was facing?

Azazel came with a horizontal swipe that was so fast it blurred the air. Raphael dodged it by arching his back and leaning backwards, but Azazel shifted the direction and came down vertically. Raphael brought both of his gauntlets up in an X block, locking Azazel's sword and stopping the progress of the blade. He kept the blade trapped there, so Azazel could move it neither up nor down. The two angels stared into each other's burning eyes, their wills locked in a gaze that would have wilted a lesser angel in an instant.

At the Portal, Lucifer was growing impatient. It was a new feeling for him. He, who had waited on God for billions of years, and waited on his own plans for years as well, was becoming annoyed at the delay of minutes. Yet it was probably not so much impatience as worry that the plan had run into a snag. He had rejoiced when he felt the three tremors that meant destruction of the Thrones, but where were the others? Had Azazel really failed him?

If he had, then there was only one solution. There were very, very few angels stronger than Azazel. Yet, none were stronger than himself. If Azazel had met his match, there was only one solution.

Lucifer himself would have to destroy the Thrones.

Although the idea was disagreeable, he had always thought in the back of his mind that it might have to be done. That was the trouble with relying on others. Eventually, they would all find a way to let him down.

Lucifer knew that there was no time to waste. He drew his sword and rushed toward the battlefield.

The distance was not long, and he covered it in nearly the speed of thought. When he got to the base of the mountain, he saw his armies swarming all around him, and they cheered as he charged forward.

"My lord!" Abbadon cried out. "Enter here to my left. The breach is largest here." Lucifer followed where Abbadon's muscular red finger was pointing and saw several of his demons in control of one of the larger openings.

"My lord!" one of them shouted. "Come through here, we have–" But what they had was never uttered, for at that moment the clean swipe of a blade destroyed the three demons with such speed that not only did they not know what hit them, they didn't even know that they had been struck.

The white-winged Michael stood in the entrance.

"Brother," Michael said, the softness in his voice at odds with the hardness of his exterior. "You shall have one last chance. Return to God now before I destroy you."

Lucifer looked for the briefest of moments as if he was considering the request, but then the light on his face faded to reveal his usual haughty features. "Let it not be said that the generosity of God is not exceeded by Lucifer. I shall likewise give you one last, but better, chance. Renounce God now and join with me, before I destroy you!"

There was no salute this time as Lucifer and Michael tore into each other. There were really no words to tell of the way they fought. Even if such words existed, the pace at which they struck out at each other was unbelievable.

Those that were there never were able to describe exactly what happened. They fought with swords, arms, legs, wings, and teeth. It seemed as if their fight itself bent time, as if several blows were struck in the same instant.

The blur broke off and the combatants separated. Lucifer struck his sword into the ground and sank to one knee to stop his slide backwards through the gravel surrounding the mountain. The crimson blade had dark clouds swirling violently like a trapped storm. The dragon's tail uncoiled and then recoiled around his hand to give him support. His shoulders hunched up over his neck and his breathing was ragged.

Michael stood over him, barely winded. He chuckled. "Did you honestly think that you, a creation of God, could fuel yourself with a power that could challenge Him? Your power is but a shadow of his."

Lucifer said nothing, but grimaced. The rest of the armies had both stopped fighting. There was no thought of all rushing in. Michael and Lucifer were so far above them that any lesser angel who tried to attack would be insignificant.

Michael stared at him, disbelief spreading on his face. "You fool. You cannot comprehend the power of God, let alone contend with it."

Lucifer had nothing else to say, and indeed, little breath to say it. But Michael's words, rather than giving Lucifer a chance to recover, enraged him all the more. Michael was embarrassing him in front of his own troops.

Lucifer tore his sword from the ground and lunged forward.

Joy in his eyes, Michael blocked the blow and swirled his sword around, wrenching Lucifer's sword from his grip. Lucifer jumped backwards, but Michael was after him.

In a blinding second, Michael had his sword at Lucifer's throat.

"It's over, Lucifer." The blade was mere atoms away from touching him. "You must now submit to God and disband your rebellion or step forward and be sent to the Containment."

Lucifer surveyed his forces out of the corner of his eye, strong, yet defeated. He looked in their eyes. Lucifer had never much cared for others, but now he felt a terrible embarrassment and feeling that he was letting them down. He looked up at his rival Seraph, standing so strong and confident. The dragon on Michael's breastplate smiled. Was it mocking him?

He could take no more. "I reject your God and I reject your choices!" Lucifer jumped back and called out to his forces as he ran. "Flee! Escape and meet at the rendezvous point!"

"Shall we give chase, sir?" Verchiel came up behind Michael's shoulder even as Michael held up his hand to halt him. "I believe we can still catch them."

"No, my friend." Michael replied. "Those are not our orders."

Backed into a corner, Raphael narrowed the gap between his forearm guards to trap Azazel's sword. Azazel struggled to wrench it free, but the Seraph was too strong.

Raphael jumped backwards and planted his feet on the wall. With a brief flutter of his brown wings that launched his body horizontally, he ran around the corner and sent both of his feet flying into Azazel's chest.

Azazel's sword clanged uselessly on the ground several feet away, but he was not finished. He sprinted towards it, with Raphael blocking the way. Azazel grabbed hold of him to grapple, but Raphael reigned down blows with his shin and arm protectors. Azazel cried out in pain after each one but would not yield. Finally, he collapsed to the floor.

"Destroy me now." Azazel's voice was little more than a whisper. It was more of a plea than a challenge.

"When you turned against God, you lost everything," Raphael spoke slowly, sadly. "You commanded before, now no one will listen to your most meager request."

Raphael reached inside of his robe and withdrew a golden cord. Azazel's eyes went wide with fear as he understood what it was made of and grasped Raphael's intention. "You can't! It will burn me. Destroy me instead! Destroy me instead!"

Alizel ran from the room then, but for the rest of his existence he would still hear Azazel's screams echoing in his mind. The cord was made of the same material as the armor, and imbued with the Father's power. The closest humans would have been able to understand was to imagine tying someone in a rope made out of pure fire.

But Raphael was not being cruel for cruelty's sake. Touching God that intimately was painful for those who had forsaken him, like putting frozen hands up to a fire. They would hurt, but the heat was the thing most needed.

Lucifer reached the Portal only seconds after his embarrassing defeat. His troops were rushing headlong and diving in, caring little that Michael's forces were not in pursuit. This was no orderly retreat. Although many of them had privately doubted Lucifer's plan all along, most had at least trusted him enough to keep fear for their own lives down deep inside. An important change had come over the hordes of demons, although none would admit it. They were not following Lucifer now because they trusted him to lead them to glory. They were now following him because they had nowhere else to go.

Lucifer grasped the railing of the Portal and took one look back at Heaven. He hesitated there for a moment. This was, really, the end of the end. He knew that once he crossed the border, he might never again return to Heaven. Yet, could he even still turn back?

"Is this what You wanted?" He screamed in the direction of the Throne of God. "Look at what has happened to us. Look at the cost of this war. Are those weak, pathetic creatures of mud worth it? Will You really pay such a price?"

You have no idea the price I pay for them.

God's words filled Heaven. Lucifer wasn't sure if he was even expecting a response, but the words certainly had an ominous tone. What could be worse than what had happened so far?

"You have already paid by losing us, every sane angel in Heaven. They will not serve this foolish plan. I will not serve them!" Although there was no need, Lucifer was screaming. Every angel in Heaven heard his words.

All must serve.

"You do not tell me what to do anymore! I have free will. I reject your offer and I reject your kingdom! You think that this is over? There are two battlefields in this war!" With his words, Lucifer flung himself over the railing with the remnant of his followers. He was gone just before he heard the Lord's last words.

All serve, Satan. Even you. Even Me.

PART THREE

CHAPTER TEN:

THE SECOND BATTLEFIELD

They drifted through limbo, stopping now and again to regroup. One by one the stragglers joined them, until Lucifer had collected most of his host around him. They were apart from the Universe, but not in Heaven either. But they were closer to Heaven than the Universe; they were still in the Realm of Spirit. Creatures of spirit needed a spiritual world.

"Where are we?" The question was asked by several demons at once. They had settled into the new location, with Lucifer's throne centered in the middle. The edges of their new domain were shifting and undefined, formless black waves that bobbed over the horizon.

Lucifer was still fuming at his defeat, and in no mood to answer. Instead Malphas, the only one of the twelve Thrones who had gone over to Lucifer's side, took over. Malphas was a pudgy demon, short and square, with a large golden hoop in each of his ears.

"We are in our new home," he replied. "Which our Lord Lucifer, in his brightness, envisioned," he added hastily. "It is not much now, but it shall become magnificent as I complete its construction. We are now in a place completely without God. Yet, it is every bit as great as Heaven."

"Shall we call it New Heaven?" Verin suggested.

"We have a name already," Malphas answered. "It is the Heaven's Equivalent Location, or HEL for short. The best thing about it is that it is transient. God cannot be here."

"I don't understand," the slow-witted Dahaka mused. "Are you saying that God cannot come here?"

"As far as we know," Malphas explained, "God can be wherever He wishes. Yet, if we don't allow Him here in our hearts, we believe that He will respect that. He has shown that much so far."

"Why should we trust what God says He will do?" Dahaka was not convinced. "He does not care what we desire."

"We cannot," Malphas admitted. "But such is the nature of the battle we face. God holds all power, save what He has granted us. Odious as it is, we have to trust His past behavior. Plus, we do have one advantage. Because HEL is the place where God isn't, if His presence intrudes upon our border, the border can shift."

"That is beautiful," Dahaka admitted rather gleefully. "So we can live together, as long as we don't let Him into our hearts. If He or His angels try to come after us, our location can shift."

"Yes. It is as dark is to light in the Universe. Dark is nothing more than the place where light is not. If the light moves, then so does the darkness."

"With our base here, we must decide now how to counterattack." Verin jumped up. "We have wasted too much time already!"

"Wasted? We have hardly spent time at all." Kasadya alone seemed barely ruffled from their ordeal. "Now is the time to regroup, and to carefully and dispassionately plan out our new strategy."

"Kasadya is right," Lucifer finally spoke, and the others turned to face him. "Although I wish to rush headlong and tear down the gates of Heaven myself, doing so would be extremely foolish. God has made His decision. He has chosen the humans over us. There is only one way to make Him pay. We will make them both pay."

"My lord!" Abbadon exclaimed. "Your brilliance shines even more brightly in our new home. Give me but the word and I will set upon them and destroy every last one of them."

Lucifer breathed in and out slowly, going over his options and keeping his own council. He stroked his chin thoughtfully with his hand. "Destroying them is good…and it will be done. But not yet. First, we must make them pay for what they have done…pay for forcing us to start this war."

"Your council is wise, my lord," Kasadya agreed. "Yet, how to make them pay? Can they be held responsible for the turmoil they have caused, as they did so unknowingly? Are we not more just—less arbitrary than God?"

"It doesn't matter!" Abbadon was ready. "Man must pay for the sins of God. Why must we worry about what is fair? Let's destroy man, Earth, the whole Universe while we are at it."

Lucifer held up a hand. "Hold, my friend. I appreciate your... enthusiasm. Kasadya's point is important, but based on a fundamental misunderstanding. It is true that the humans did not know of what they caused nor choose willfully to cause it. In fairness, we should not destroy them. However, that is assuming that the humans are our equals. The humans are nothing to us. They have the faintest spark of the divine within them, but are still creatures of matter. We are creatures of spirit. Their lifetime is a flicker compared to our billions of years of existence. Our knowledge surpasses theirs by an equal margin. Their minds are feeble and grasp even the simplest of ideas with great difficulty. No, the humans are not our equals and are not to be treated as such."

Lucifer looked around. Most of the demons were slowly nodding their heads.

"If any one of you needs more proof, see how they treat those lower than them. Look at their lives before God gave them souls. Does a man feel the need to be fair to an ant? Does or does he not rip a fruit from a tree to satisfy his wants? Who among you can say that man deserves anything different from us?"

There was a rumble of agreement. Lucifer's case was not a hard one to make. Every last demon there was lusting for someone to blame for their position. By reasoning through the argument, he kept them believing that what they were doing was right.

"So if we are not to destroy them now, what then shall we do?" Abbadon's massive bulk seemed crestfallen at the loss of his sport.

"That's easy," Lucifer answered. "We'll make God regret the day He ever created them."

Eve rolled over to stare up at the sun and let its rays wash over the front of her body. It was a glorious afternoon, the kind where she didn't mind being alone with her thoughts. The warmth of the sun felt delightful as it spread all throughout her muscles and skin. She remembered an opposite sensation, but couldn't place it. It was a dream within a dream, something from her former life that wasn't even a life, really. Cold, fear, and pain had no place here in Eden.

She couldn't say that she missed the old life, not in the least. But what if this new life was also an old life for something else? The idea bothered her. What had she done to move from the old life to this one? She didn't know that it was of no merit of her own, that God had breathed a part of His life into her and had thus turned her from animal to human. She had no conception of it, and couldn't imagine herself as an animal. Animals weren't thoughtful. Animals were different than humans. This idea was firmly planted in her mind.

That's what made it so surprising when she heard one speak.

"Eve," it said. Eve started and looked all around, initially unable to find the speaker.

"Adam?" She didn't think it was her husband, but the only beings that she had heard speak were him, the Lord, and the other humans.

"Down here," it hissed. "It is I, the serpent."

Eve crouched down and looked into the serpent's face. At the back of her mind a primal instinct told her to be afraid of such a creature, but fear had no place here.

"Hello, little serpent," Eve answered him. "How is it that you talk? Are you God?"

The serpent spat and hissed. "No, my friend. I am better than God."

Eve was taken aback. "Better than God? How can such a thing be possible? He has created this whole garden, and He has created us."

"He has created you," the serpent admitted, "although the task was small. Dear child, do you not yearn for more? I can give you so much more that you would look upon your current condition with disgust and shame."

"I... I do not know what those words mean." Eve was a little embarrassed. She had never heard those words before.

"There is much that you do not know. I could tell you, but then you would not know other things."

"Can you tell me the things that I don't know?"

"I could tell you some of them," the serpent replied. "But you still would not know what you didn't know. Say that you knew ten things, how would you know if there were a hundred things to know or a thousand?"

Eve's face showed that the idea was troublesome to her. "Could you tell me how many things there are to know?"

"Certainly, I could. Yet the number is so high that you do not have words for it. I could tell you things for years and years and years, and still there would be far more to know."

Eve's expression grew more and more troubled, and then light again.

"If that is the case, then we must not be meant to know everything. I do not believe that God would have created us to be unhappy."

"Oh, but you are wrong. I said that I could not tell you everything, but there is a fruit in this very garden which can show you it all in an instant. All it takes is one little bite."

"What fruit is this? I have been up and down this garden, and have tasted no such fruit."

"But have you tasted every fruit?"

Eve was confused again. "Yes, I believe that we have."

"You haven't tasted the fruit from the tree in the center."

"That fruit? That's not for us. The Lord specifically told us not to eat it."

"I see," said the snake, nodding his head up and down. "And why do you think that the Lord told you this?"

Eve was having trouble with the question. Although she was naturally much more inquisitive than Adam, the idea of questioning why God did anything had clearly not occurred to her.

"Well..." She started, broke off to think, and then began again. "Perhaps because it's not good for us to eat."

"Has he told you not to eat anything else that is not good for you? Has he commanded you not to eat the bark of the tree, or the rocks of the field?"

"No... I guess that I just never thought to eat those things. We just kind of know that they aren't for eating."

"Well, the fruit of this tree *is* different," said the snake. "Would you like to know how?"

Eve said nothing but her eyes betrayed her. It was obvious that she wanted to know very badly. How could one fruit be so different from the others?

The snake turned to slither away. "When you want to find out, come find me."

Kasadya sat on a rock and took in the situation around him. Their life was to be so different now. The demons in HEL were closely monitoring the events in Eden, but with Lucifer gone, there was no clear command structure. Although Baal Zebub was technically in charge, even he wouldn't order anything other than waiting. There was no point in setting up fortifications with the shifting border, although they were closely monitoring it and had three lines of lower ranking soldiers ready on the perimeter should Michael and his forces try to attack.

Out of nowhere, a horrible scream rent the air. The demons turned toward the sound, drawing their swords to face off against an assault from Heaven's angels.

There was no attack, however. The screaming mass hit the floor and rolled. The demons circled it to see what it was, and it was immediately clear.

It was one of them.

It was Azazel.

He rolled around on the ground, screaming out at his bonds. "Someone get me out of here!"

Verin rushed forward to tear at the bonds and then screamed himself.

"I can't touch this!" He wrung his hands trying to get the sting off. "What is this made of?"

"It came from Raphael. The essence of *Him*!" Azazel spat the name, struggling and rolling in agony.

The demons all looked at him, none knowing quite what to do. They had never seen something like this before.

"We had better wait for Lucifer," Kasadya suggested. "He may know how to defeat this horrible bondage."

No one stepped forward to suggest anything different. They wouldn't back down when facing one of Michael's troops, but none dared to touch the rope made from the essence of God.

One by one the demons walked away, leaving Azazel alone with his screams.

Eve didn't go back to see the serpent the next day, or the day after. She kept going over what he had told her in her mind, tossing around the possibilities and letting them settle. Every time she passed by the tree, it seemed to be a little more exciting. The fruits glistened with the morning dew. What would it be like to know everything?

She wondered why God had put a tree there if they were not to eat from it. Was it just to tempt them? So far, what she had known about God showed that He wouldn't be like that. Why then?

An odd thought struck her. What if God had put the tree there as a test for her and Adam? As she thought about it, the test could go both ways. Maybe God wanted them to do something to earn their knowledge. Maybe knowledge was special, and that is why it had to be earned, while food, water, sunshine, and everything else was just given to them.

But, the reverse could be true as well. What if knowledge wasn't the important thing? What if the tree was just there to test their obedience? What if the tree didn't give knowledge at all? What if it was just a regular tree and God desired their obedience over all?

As she thought about the second possibility, it seemed the more "real" to her. She wasn't aware of it, but this was the first time a human being used her conscience. Although His actions weren't provable by science, He nevertheless gave each human being a special compass that oriented towards His will at all times. He did not impinge on their free will, but did still give them a connection to Him so they could discern between good and evil.

The serpent slithered up from the grass next to her. It slid around her heels, and she felt a chill run up her spine. Eve shivered, something that she had not done since her ensoulment. The snake shot away. She wondered if the experience hadn't been more unpleasant for him.

"What was that feeling?" Eve asked. Although she felt danger, she couldn't really articulate what it was.

"It was nothing," the serpent hissed. "My scales are cold and do not feel good against your bare skin."

Eve wasn't sure that that was it, but she let it go. The serpent was watching the tree, seeing that none of the fruit had been broken from their stems.

"If that tree is so special to you, why don't you eat the fruit yourself?" The question was out almost before Eve intended it to be, but it did make sense to her. Indeed, why hadn't the serpent tasted any of the fruit of that tree? Another thought came into her mind. "How do you know so much about this tree anyway?"

"The answers to your questions are both related," the serpent replied. "Indeed, I have already shared in the knowledge of this tree." He seemed to falter for the briefest second before continuing. "I have shared this knowledge, and thus am I able to speak with you. Have you heard any other beast of the earth or air stop to converse with you? Has the hare of the field given you precious secrets? I think not. I alone can show you the way to your future."

It was true. No other creature besides humans and the Lord had ever come to speak with her. Perhaps this snake had tasted of the tree.

"Why do I wish you to eat of it? In a word, pity. I pity you for your limited sight of God's beautiful creation.

"If you do eat it," the snake continued on, "you really don't have anything to lose. If there is a problem later, you will be able to solve it with the knowledge that you have gained."

It made sense to Eve. If she just took one little bite and she wasn't supposed to, she would have the knowledge to know what to do next.

"Although I wish you to share in this knowledge, and I wish you to see as I see, it doesn't matter to me whether you eat it or not. Perhaps I should just find some of the other humans or even other creatures and tell them the secret. In fact, I think I'll do that tomorrow."

"No, wait!" Eve cried out. The thought of losing the chance to attain all that knowledge, of losing out while others ate from the tree was almost more than she could bear.

"I'll do it."

The snake hissed his pleasure. "All it takes in one little bite. I came to you first because God created you and Adam before the others. But if you're not a changed woman by tomorrow morning, I will have to find someone else more worthy."

Trembling, Eve inched her way towards the tree.

Alizel was down at the Portal, watching Earth. Most of the angels were there, or strolling through the rebuilt Heaven.

It hadn't taken more than a fraction of a second after Lucifer left before God's glory burned throughout all Heaven, removing all traces of Lucifer's rebellion and restoring their lovely home to its former splendor. It was as if the rebellion had never happened. The streams of liquid diamond once again flowed freely from one side of the kingdom to the other. The gardens were once again filled with brilliant hues, mixing in patterns no human eye has seen and no human pen could describe. Angels strolled freely and without fear.

The only one who wasn't completely healed was Eleleth. Although her body seemed fine and she was able to get out of bed and walk around with the other angels, for some reason she was not made whole. Her wings were gone, the feathers tattered to the point where they simply fell off. Angels took them and placed them on an altar in a temple close to Mt. Zion. Alizel wondered if she would ever soar again.

Although Heaven looked the same physically, it was taking a while for the angels to get used to the changes. Nothing Lucifer had done could mar even the slightest part of God's creation. But inside, the angels were hurting. God hadn't opened up the Containment yet. Alizel wondered why. There were bad angels as well as good ones in there. But somehow that didn't seem like it was it. Alizel had no doubt that He could destroy it and let the trapped angels free, but He didn't. One of the more radical theories circulating around was that holding the angels from the war wasn't even the main purpose of the Containment in the first place. There was even a rumor that God had put something else into the Containment. Alizel couldn't imagine what else He was using it for.

Alizel checked himself and nearly laughed out loud at that last thought he had had. As if he even dared to imagine the plans of God! If one thing was for certain, it was that His plans were far broader and far deeper than anything angels could imagine.

The hierarchy was reorganized, but only to take advantage of those angels who had left. Thus Uriel was still his Principality, and Katel was still his Archangel, even though he was in the Containment. This gave Alizel great hope to see him once again.

Alizel never would have guessed that everything revolved around the humans. *Why* were they so important? Lucifer was right about how small they were. Alizel wondered if they even knew of the angels' existence. Or, if they could even comprehend their existence, if they did know about it. Perhaps part of their importance was not only in spite of their limitations, but because of their limitations.

Angels had all been trained in how to interact with the Universe, of course, and Alizel saw it backfiring already. Entranced, he watched from the Portal. Lucifer was entering into Eve's brain, manipulating the subatomic particles there and making her see the image of a serpent. He manipulated the neurons in the auditory pathways leading to her brain so that she thought she was engaging it in conversation.

How had God overlooked this? Surely He must have known something like this could happen. Interacting with the Universe wasn't a trivial thing for angels, but neither was it too difficult.

Lucifer could have even created a snake or transformed himself into one, although such a feat would have been far more difficult than merely altering the reality Eve experienced. Did God know that Lucifer would have figured it out?

What was Lucifer hoping to accomplish? Surely he could introduce disease into the humans or even kill them with little effort. Why was he content to just talk with them? As Alizel pondered the question, he thought he already knew the answer.

Lucifer wasn't interested in destroying their bodies. He was after their souls.

CHAPTER ELEVEN:

THE FALL OF MAN

The fruit was so beautiful. Iridescent hues shimmered along its surface. Eve felt a terrible longing to reach out and pluck one. She surveyed the different fruits. Each one seemed so close to the others. It didn't really matter which one she took.

Even as she felt the longing, her conscience was screaming inside of her not to take it, to reconsider or even ask Adam about it. But she knew that it wouldn't stop her. The tree was hypnotic.

Her arm almost had a mind of its own, reaching out and grasping the fruit. She felt an electric thrill when her hand contacted the skin. She caressed it for a moment and then pulled down quickly. The stem gave almost no resistance. It was if it wanted her to eat it.

She raised it slowly to her chin and opened her mouth. She pushed it gingerly against her teeth, depressing the skin of the fruit softly. Her mouth was salivating like never before. Her mind yearned for answers.

She bit down.

Images spun inside Eve's mind. She saw people, thousands upon thousands of them, but looking strange. They had all kinds of colored things hanging on their bodies. She saw large and small balls rotating. She saw the mysteries of the Universe, the inside of cells, the secrets of the atom. She saw the future and the past. She was terrified at the depths of evil, and saw the power of good, of sacrifice. She saw all this and more, but it was far beyond her comprehension.

She tore herself away from the fruit, biting down hard and almost choking as she swallowed. There had been so much there, but it had all happened so fast. Already, mere seconds later, she had forgotten most of what she had seen.

She looked around her. Somehow the world was different. She saw no sign of the snake. Had he betrayed her? How would she now feel when she looked upon the snake again?

Something else was different. Why had those other people been wearing things like animals wore fur?

Was there something wrong with her skin?

The snake had promised her knowledge, and the fruit had over delivered. So why did she feel like she knew and understood so much less than before? What was this great sadness she felt weighing down on her heart?

It was a feeling like nothing she had felt since the Lord had put a piece of His spirit inside of her. Yet, somehow, she knew what to call it.

What Eve didn't know was that the sadness she felt was the result of tens of thousands of angels weeping, an emotion so powerful and mournful that it crossed the barrier between the worlds.

She brought the fruit to her lips and took another bite to quell the rising panic all the questions were causing inside of her. Her mind was again assaulted with far more images and facts than she could even begin to comprehend. Taking another bite and yet another did not help.

What could she do now? The fruit was half eaten, but the knowledge she could understand was only the tiniest fraction of what there was to know. It was like trying to drink the ocean a wave at a time.

She looked around for the snake again but he was still not there. She tried to call out to him, and then realized that she didn't even know his name. The back of her mind told her to search out God, that He alone could make things right. But, somehow, she felt that even He couldn't fix this.

There was only one thing left to do. She had to go to Adam.

Adam looked up as Eve arrived. He could immediately tell that something was wrong with her. He didn't know if she was more like an animal or more like something else. Her eyes looked ragged, scared almost, but there was a new depth to them. It confused him greatly.

"Eve, my dear. What has happened to you?"

Eve came up to him and held him tight. "It wasn't what happened, but what I did."

"You did this?" Adam was surprised. "What could you possibly do that would make you like this?"

"I... I ate a fruit. It came from the Tree of Knowledge."

"Eve!" Adam was aghast. "He told us never to eat from that tree! What would cause you to do such a thing?"

Where before Eve wasn't sure what to make of what she had done, now Adam's tone made her defensive. "Well, I haven't died. Besides, a snake told me to eat it. He said that the Tree had all knowledge in it, if I just ate the fruit I would see everything and know everything."

Adam's curiosity was piqued for the first time. "And what did you see?"

"I don't know. I saw many, many things. But they all happened so quickly that I don't remember anything."

Adam nodded his head. "I understand." It was clear he didn't.

"No, you don't!" Eve was adamant. "You can't understand until you try it too!"

"You want me to eat it too? But what about what God said?"

"He said we would die if we ate it, but I haven't died. I've gotten knowledge."

Adam wasn't convinced. "What kind of knowledge do we need? Don't we know all we need to already?"

Eve grabbed Adam around the shoulders and shook him. "No, don't you see? There is so much to learn, so much to know! But you can't see it until you eat the fruit too."

Adam thought about it for only a moment, and then agreed. "If it means that much to you, then I'll eat it too."

Eve took one of the fruits from behind her back and gave it to Adam.

Adam bit down.

Eve watched Adam. This time she saw the effects of the fruit from the outside rather than the inside. She saw him chew and swallow, saw the look that came over his face, and understood that he was seeing something very similar to what she had experienced. His mind was also being overwhelmed with all the knowledge. He probably understood even less than she did.

In that moment, she knew that they had made a terrible mistake. The snake had not lied to them, really. He had said what the fruit was, what it could show them. He just had failed to mention that they would not be able to understand what they saw.

Eve was anxious. When Adam returned to himself, she spoke to him.

"What did you see?"

Adam was almost at a loss for words. "I saw so much... people, places, animals... strange things.... good things, and something else... this must be Evil."

"I know what you mean," Eve answered, looking around to see if any of those things had crept into the garden.

"Is that why they are Evil? Because they were brought by you, Eve?"

Adam's words stung Eve. She hadn't brought those things! She was just as frightened of them as Adam was!

Though his words were unfair, they stuck. While the knowledge gained from the tree was both good and evil, with unprepared minds the two were frightened.

"What should we do about them now?"

"We can't let anyone see us like this." Adam's response was almost automatic. "And we can't let God know what we have done. We have to hide."

Adam's statement left a deep sorrow in Alizel's heart as he watched from the Portal. At times, he had begun to think of humans as more than they were. What was saddest was not Adam and Eve's shame, but the fact that Adam knew so little about his maker as to think that hiding from Him would do any good whatsoever. If Adam, who had walked and talked with God in the cool shadows of the Garden, knew God so little, how much less would future generations of humanity understand Him?

Alizel could see that Eve had begun to realize just how mistaken she was in thinking that the Tree of Knowledge would teach them how to respond to every situation. After all, it wasn't called the Tree of Wisdom. She had made the all too common mistake of confusing one with the other. In this she could not really be faulted. Lucifer, after all, had made the same mistake. He had a supreme amount of knowledge, just not much wisdom to go with it.

He watched as Adam and Eve ran through the underbrush until they came through a place where the trees were thicker around the base. They ripped off branches and tore up grass, trying to make a place where they could conceal themselves. Of course, it would not have taken an experienced tracker to know that something was hiding in the undergrowth, and nothing they could ever do could hide them from God.

Almost as soon as they had hidden, the Portal opened up in front of him and Alizel turned to see the full Cherubim honor guard going through it.

He cringed for Adam and Eve's sake. What would the Father do? They had disobeyed His direct order. There was really no getting around that fact. Would He simply destroy them and start over? Would He give the humans the same fate as He had given Lucifer? Or would He simply abandon them and let natural forces take their course?

He spun around again and watched the confrontation he knew was coming.

Lucifer was there to meet God's presence as He filled the entire Universe.

"My Lord," Lucifer stood without bowing. "You know why I am here."

Speak.

"I have shown You the weakness of the humans. The first two have both turned away from You. You cannot say that they still deserve their special place in Your creation." Lucifer's words were bold, yet not spiteful. The challenge he put to God was remarkable.

What they have, they have because I choose to give. They have never deserved it.

"Yet they have rejected Your gift. They have chosen themselves over You. They have chosen, as have many of Your created angels, to believe in their own reason and their own light. By right of their disobedience, these humans and their offspring belong to me."

Alizel's hands tightened on the railing as he watched.

God said nothing, so Lucifer continued.

"The Lord is just and merciful, it is said." Lucifer was ready with his cornerstone point. "Yet you cannot now be both. By rights of justice, they have eaten the fruit and must die. Just as I paid the penalty for my...sin, so must they. If you show mercy, then you deny justice. If you show justice, you deny mercy. Which will it be?"

As you have said, We are just and merciful. The penalty is not erased. Yet, they shall not be yours.

"How can this be, Lord?" Lucifer was furious. "The debt must be paid!"

The Lord was silent for just a moment.

Because I pay the debt Myself.

172

CHAPTER TWELVE:

THE PROMISE

Adam, Adam, where are you?

The Lord was calling out to him. Alizel might have laughed, were it not for the seriousness of the situation. Imagine, God who knew every quark of every atom of the Universe, was asking where Adam was. But he wasn't asking for Himself, to learn the answer. He was asking for Adam, to make him say it.

Whether or not Adam realized this, he was at least smart enough to know that hiding from God was not going to cause God to forget about him.

"I was hiding, Lord." He came out and bowed his head.

Why were you hiding from Me?

"I'm sorry, Lord... but I was ashamed." Alizel could tell that Adam was hoping God would guess his indiscretion, or offer healing right away. But Alizel knew that God was going to make him say it.

What were you ashamed of, My child?

"I ate a fruit from the Tree of Knowledge."

God did not reply for a moment, and in that time Adam spoke again.

"It was the woman who you put here with me," he said quickly. "She ate it first and then came and told me to eat it as well."

"I am sorry, Lord," she said. "It's true. But the serpent tricked me into eating it. He said that we would not die. Will you kill us now?"

My child, all that I tell you must be. The death that I warned you against is of a different kind. While you were here in this Garden, you could have lived forever. But because of the sin that both of you have committed, you must all now leave this place. Yes, Eve, you will die. Not today, and not for many years, but one day it must come.

"We must leave here? But where will we go?" Eve asked.

Alizel wondered if to the human, it almost seemed like death might be better.

You must go out into the world. Where before, the earth worked for you, now you must work the earth. By the sweat of your brow you will live. I will seal this Garden, and none may enter.

It was Adam who spoke up next. "Lord, will we never know You again? Can we ever make what has happened right?"

Adam, I am yours, and you are Mine, for always. Nothing can ever change this. I will be with you and your descendants whenever you call on Me. I am there in the heat of the day and the cool of the morning, whenever you seek after My ways. Believe me when I tell you that there is nothing you can do to make this right, but today I make a Promise to you. One day I will send Someone who can.

It was the first that Alizel had heard of this. His brows narrowed in confusion. And what was this about God paying the debt Himself? Why wouldn't He just forgive the debt?

Adam looked at Eve, and she looked back at him. They didn't say anything but slowly started to walk toward the border of Eden. They had never thought of leaving Eden before, or even of Eden having a border. How could they walk out into the unknown?

They started walking, mindlessly, still numb over what was happening to them and what they had lost. Soon they came to a large wall, with a hole in it where they could see out into the rest of the world. The land next to Eden was still bountiful, but something just didn't look right about it to Eve.

The other humans in the Garden came up to the gateway with them. Adam and Eve's minds raced with questions and doubt. Was it fair for them all to have to leave? Would any of them have been able to resist the lure of the fruit, or would they all have fallen sooner or later?

Were all humans born fallible, with a propensity towards sin? If so, how could they hope to live their lives spotlessly?

What would happen to their souls when their bodies could no longer sustain them?

As they started moving out of Eden, the land around them changed. The trees grew less lush, the vegetation dried up, and the fruits started to grow more and more sparse. It was evening, and as they had no particular place to go, they started walking West towards the setting sun. It seemed right for them to walk that way. Walking towards the rising sun seemed the right thing to do in a time of new beginnings.

Adam did not know how long they walked. They stumbled numbly along, unable to replay the events of the last few hours. The events would be replayed over and over throughout human history, but for now, he did not want to think about what they had done.

Their little band of humans walked for days and days, not stopping to rest or eat. Adam did not know that the last of Eden's food was nourishing their bodies. They had never felt hunger before in Eden, and soon it was overbearing. They stopped their journey long enough to find some berries and drink from a spring. Having to find food and water was a big change from Eden. Before, whatever they wanted was there for them immediately.

One night along their journey raindrops started to fall from the heavens, soaking their skin and chilling them straight through. Adam searched around him for a place to be dry, and suddenly his eyes came upon a cave hewn into the rock face up ahead. Adam pointed it out to Eve, and they were nearly suffering from hypothermia by the time they made it.

Exhausted, and clinging to each other for warmth, they lay on the cave floor and fell asleep.

Orifel, head of the Thrones and Michael, head of the Seraphim, hovered in the air near the two glowing stars. The stars were a pair orbiting close to each other. They had been sent directly by God Himself, to make a sign in the sky for the Promise that God the Father was making in Eden, nearly eighty light years away.

Time seemed to stand still as the two watched the events unfolding on Earth, but when the Promise was made, they knew the time had come. As things were now, the stars would be nothing more than luminous balls of plasma, bursting forth with nuclear fusion, no different than the trillions of others in the Universe.

Yet God had different plans for these two stars.

Michael turned to Orifel and nodded, a smile coming to his lips as starlight reflected in his eyes. Orifel returned the signal, and Michael could tell that his friend understood his meaning immediately.

Orifel turned into a huge wheel, nearly the size of the star itself, and spun toward its surface. He sliced through the star, his energy breaking the bonds of gravity that held it together. Flames burst out from all sides, as each part of the star flew away from the other.

Michael was waiting, bringing his hands up and to the sides, palms turned inwards towards each other. Michael increased in size too, taking one of the star halves and pushing it together, molding the half-sphere into a smaller sphere, to be its own small orange star. Such was the strength of Michael that he did not show the slightest exertion from the effort of molding a star. He then turned to the other half star, pushing it together as well, and letting it give off a crimson glow. There were now three stars orbiting close to each other.

Orifel then turned to the second, brighter star. He sliced through again, this time not dividing them evenly, but keeping one large star and one smaller one. Michael molded the first, taking away most of its energy and leaving a small, massive and dim star – a dense white dwarf. The bigger part, nearly four times as massive as Earth's Sun yet four hundred times as bright, he let burn as a blue-white star. The two stars whirled around each other.

Michael smiled, pleased with his work. If anyone had noticed, they would have seen four distinct stars that in themselves held a message for the future. The small orange star represented the fire of the Holy Spirit that would come down. The simmering red star foretold the blood that would flow. The largest and brightest blue-white star was a symbol of the living waters that would wash away sins, and finally, the small dense white dwarf star was the sign of a death without sin.

The four stars were made of two pairs of two stars each which danced with their partner as well as the other pair. Yet the stars were so far from Earth that when sages glanced up at the night sky with the naked eye they would see but a single bright point. The star was the brightest point by far in the constellation of The Lion. Over time it would be known by all cultures on earth by various names, Basiliscus, Qalb Al Asad, Alpha Leonis, the Yellow Emperor, Venant or simply Regulus – the King Star.

Michael checked the sizes and positions of the stars and went over his calculations again. They were perfectly positioned to be in the right place thousands of years in the future, where they would rise in the sky above Earth, over a stable.

Two figures strolled through the Garden, one a little in front of the other. Alizel had remained by the Portal as the humans journeyed, his heart aching in sympathy for them. Now, he watched these two figures curiously, wondering what they intended to do in the humans' former abode.

They walked causally, with no particular destination. It was as if they had all the time in the world, which, in fact, they did. They examined each tree, and every blossom of every flower, as if to more fully understand what Adam and Eve had given up.

It could have been days or weeks, but eventually they reached their destination. A wall spread out around the Garden, encompassing it. But that was far from the necessary protection.

"Jophiel, thank you for agreeing to this assignment." One spoke to the other, his voice calm and without pretext.

The Cherub bowed low. "You know I exist solely to serve my Lord."

The other nodded. "Your service is much appreciated." He brought His hand up, clenched His fist, and drew a sword out of thin air. He spun the sword and handed it to Jophiel, who amazingly, was not shocked at the existence of such a weapon.

"I will withdraw Eden from the Realm of Matter, so that no humans will again enter. Our Adversary, however, can come here, so I have given you this weapon."

Suddenly, it was plain to Alizel who the other figure was. He marveled at the form his Lord had chosen to take on. While all angels did things humans would find hard to believe, only One could create. Not rearrange atoms, or bring something out that was hidden, but really create, bring something forth out of nothing. God the Son was a manifestation of the Trinity in human form, yet He was not particularly tall or strong. He was God, yet He had subjected himself to the physical laws of the Universe in taking a body.

The youth-faced Cherub nodded and bowed again. "Thank you, Lord." He did not question how he would defend against all of Lucifer's hordes. As a rule, Jophiel did not question anything, ever. He had learned that God answered all his questions in time.

God the Son continued. "This weapon is different from the others. While the other weapons could strike in only one direction and one place at a time, this sword contains My omnipresence. Therefore, no matter how many attack you, this sword can strike in all directions simultaneously."

Jophiel took a step back in awe as he watched a burst of energy suddenly flare up the edge of the sword. For one who trusted God completely and was never surprised at His marvels, even this was almost too much. He bowed low again. "You honor me with this task."

God the Son smiled. "You wish to know something more."

"Yes, my Lord. There are many things that I wish to know, but I trust that You will reveal everything to me in Your time."

"You see the extreme power of this weapon, and wish to know why the war continued so long when one strike from such a weapon could have ended it."

"My Lord, the war could have been ended by this weapon, a blow from Your Mighty Fist, or a single Word spoken from Your Lips. It matters little which. The war continued because it was not Your Will to stop it. There is no other explanation."

"You are right, of course," God the Son replied. "All things move according to Our Will, and it is Our Will to allow others to have free will as well. But you wonder why We allowed the war, why Heaven was rent until all angels wept."

Alizel felt the tension. This was the one question no one had ever been able – or willing – to answer. He leaned forward on the railing, hoping at long last to understand.

Jophiel said nothing, so God the Son continued. "The service you give to Us is freely given, and deeply appreciated. Yet you were created to know, as you were created to serve. The humans have only a spark of Us inside of them. The faith We wish from them is of a different kind. We wish them to make a real choice between Good and Evil. In order to make that choice, there must be those who pull them away from Us. We look for their choice in the midst of doubt. You must know Darkness to love Light."

Jophiel nodded again. "Even Lucifer fulfills Your Will, although he believes himself to make his own destiny. That is why You called him Satan when he was leaving Heaven."

"Yes. Satan is not a name, but merely a title. He has now taken on the role of the Adversary of humans and angels. Heaven was lost to him as a natural result of his actions, as it must be for everyone. Yet, even his evil is no match for Our grace, if he could but ask for it. It is true that he fulfills Our Will, as all beings must. We must all serve…no matter the cost."

With His last statement, God the Son saluted Jophiel and turned away into the center of the Garden.

He stared at the Tree rising up before Him, its branches twisting outwards from the center. Crimson blossoms shot out along the length of not only the branches but also the trunk as well. The roots branched out deeply through the cool earthy soil, drawing nutrients from the rest of the Garden. This Tree was near the other Tree, and intertwined with it throughout human history.

A triumphant sadness hung in the air, as if the Tree had some vague memory of the future. God the Son slowly approached it, letting His hand come up and gently caress the wood. All times were one for the One who had created time. He could travel forward and backwards through time as others traveled through space. In contrast to His angels, He alone had access to all dimensions of the space-time continuum. He gave people and angels free will to make their choices and shape the future, while also knowing ahead of time what they would choose.

God the Son allowed Himself to travel forward in time in His mind, to when He would again meet with the Tree of Life. Pain suddenly exploded through His body and His mind reeled.

The only sign on the outside was a single tear that came down His face.

EPILOGUE

So now you have heard the beginning of my story. Mankind had its first encounter with Lucifer, and emerged defeated. It was only after much thought on the matter that I realized the intricacy of the situation. Of course, God was stronger, much stronger, than Lucifer. Yet, Lucifer and his demons were much stronger than mankind, upon whom everything rested.

Realizing that, the path for us angels was clear. It was our job to oppose Lucifer, to fight him and his minions in the little daily battles. God had told us to stay on the sidelines for Lucifer's first battle with the humans. It tore me up inside to watch Lucifer talking to Eve, powerless to do anything.

I saw Lucifer's persuasion techniques. It wasn't too long ago that he was doing the same thing to all of us in Heaven. Perhaps that's the only reason I recognized them when he used them on the humans. I like to think that I was smarter than that, but he had fooled even us. People think that Lucifer lies all the time. Sure, he's deceitful, but he very rarely lies. Lies are too easy to detect.

No, as in the case of Eve, Lucifer tells the truth. He just doesn't tell all of it, and he adds just a little falsehood to it. He weaves a mixture of truth, flattery, and prodding into something very believable.

I doubt Eve realized all of this at the time, or even knew who Lucifer was. Through our efforts and Lucifer's, her descendants would come to know it all too well.

God was still in the Universe, but it wasn't the same. It wasn't like He wasn't there anymore, because He was always everywhere. But He wasn't in the Universe in the same way as He was when He was speaking with Adam. I know you probably don't understand what I mean by that, and it's hard to explain. You'll just have to take my word for it.

The war in Heaven was really only the beginning. The battle lines were drawn, the pieces all on the board. In my mind I wondered who among us would be able to stand up to Lucifer — in my heart I knew it would always have to be Michael.

Raphael and Azazel fought the first of many battles they would have in the millennia to come. I must say that I, indeed everyone, was shocked that Azazel turned. But I guess all the defectors had their own reasons. For him I think it was more about the weapons than anything, and the power that they gave him. He loved the power even more than he loved God. Although...sometimes I wondered if strength wasn't really a weakness. It seemed like the strongest, most warlike angels were especially vulnerable to failure.

After Azazel was cast out, Verchiel took over as head of the Powers, and became the angel responsible for keeping us safe from external assault. Verchiel created an internal police to monitor things inside of Heaven, and set an angel named Quenten up to be in charge of this important division.

Perhaps the saddest part of the story concerns the angel Oliver. He had been forced to use hate, yet once he had used it he had been unable to turn away from his new way of thinking completely. We found out later that he left Heaven, but for some reason did not join up with Lucifer in HEL. If anything, somehow he was trapped in the middle. Although I mourned his loss, I had faith that somehow, some day he would be able to find his way back.

Truly, our Father was amazing. I couldn't wait to see what would happen next.

SCENE FROM ANGEL WARS SAGA
BOOK TWO:

The fire on the inside of the tent shone forth as its tongues writhed and danced with the beat of the music coming from within. The lone stranger listened outside for a brief moment before stepping inside. He was clean shaven, with black hair parted over the middle and piercing blue eyes the color of deep sky. He was of average height and average build, and wore a loose cloak that hung evenly from his body. He was no one you would happen to remember.

At least, that's the image he projected into the minds of all the humans who were nearby.

The man reached a gloved hand up and parted the entrance flap to the tent, stepping inside. He surveyed the scene to the left and to the right. The men and women in the tent were enjoying themselves, drinking a beer made from fermented barley through reed straws. Several of the revelers were barely clothed, and their minds were clouded by the effects of the drink. They were singing and laughing, most of them oblivious to the one who had entered. For this moment, at least, they were freed from the cares and toils of the world.

All of them, that is, except for one. A lone hooded figure sat in the corner, his drink unshared and untouched. His features were dark and his face was troubled. The stranger smiled.

"Excuse me," he said, stopping a man who was engaged with a giggling girl. The man paid little attention. "What's with that one over there?"

His question caused the man and the girl to stop and really look at him for the first time. "Friend, if you have any concern for yourself, leave that man alone."

"Is he dangerous, then?"

"You have no idea. Dangerous, and in a bad mood tonight. Believe me, friend. You're much better off to find a pretty girl and a drink and leave that man be."

The stranger nodded his head and concluded the conversation. "I thank you for your kind advice," he said, ignoring the man and walking directly towards the hooded figure.

The stranger sat down next to the man who was staring sullenly into the fire. He had sunken, haunted eyes. His beard was uneven with pink splotches and scabs where he had plucked parts of it.

"It's quite the party, isn't it?" The stranger started. The man pretended not to hear and the stranger couldn't help but smile. He had, after all, not spoken out loud, but manipulated the very electrical impulses in the man's cochlear nerve.

"I said, it's quite the party!" This time when he spoke, he pushed the man around the shoulder, giving him no excuse to further ignore him.

The hooded man brushed the stranger's hand away, his eyes suddenly turning menacing. "Don't you know who I am?"

"Yes I do, Cain."

"Then you should know not to touch me."

Was it a warning, or remorse that made him feel unworthy of human contact?

"I want to know something, of you, Cain. Did you feel power when you did it? Did you enjoy the feeling that no one can force anything from you?"

For the first time, Cain seemed to be actually listening. A darkness began building behind his eyes as the love of the power crept into his face. For as much as he hated himself for it, and as much as he would never admit it to anyone who didn't already understand— he *had* enjoyed the feeling it gave him.

"What do you want from me?"

"It's simple, really. I want to teach you how to do it right. Not with crude stones, but with weapons— real weapons. Things that can make it so easy that even a child can do it."

The stranger looked into Cain's astonished yet hungry face. "My name is Azazel, and we have much work to do."

CHARACTER LIST

SERAPHIM

Seraphim, or "Flaming Ones" are the highest ranking order of angels. Secretive and powerful, they rule over the other orders of angels. They wear a platinum sash with a crimson S.

Luciferel/Lucifer – *"The Bright One of God/The Bright One"* – Luciferel was the highest ranking angel in Heaven, who eventually changes his own name when he casts off God's Energy and takes over the rebellion.

Raphael – *"God Heals"* – Raphael is one of the leading Seraphim and the nemesis of Azazel.

Michael – *"Who is like the Lord"* – Michael is the general of the Armies of God. His nemesis is Lucifer.

Gabriel – *"Strong Man of God"* – Gabriel is a powerful Seraph whose chief duty is managing the flow of information in Heaven.

CHERUBIM

Cherubim are the second order of angels. They spend all their time and energy in direct worship and take only a passing interest in the affairs of the other angels. They have a white sash with a gold C.

Ophaniel – Leader of the Cherubim

Jophiel – "*God's Beauty*" – Cherubim angel set to guard Eden with an omni-directional flaming sword.

Selaphiel – "*Prayer of God*"

Jehudiel – "*Glorifying of God*" – Head of worshiping in Heaven.

Camael – "*He who sees God*" – Angel of pure love.

Hanael – "*Joy of God*"

THRONES
The Thrones are great teachers and also responsible for the structure of the spiritual realm. The Thrones wear an earthy brown sash with a green T.

Orifel – Head of the Thrones.

Bodiel – Throne angel and head teacher.

Malphas – Builder and destroyer demon. Later helps Lucifer to construct HEL.

DOMINIONS
Angels who are in charge of a particular nation, group of humans, or physical feature on the Earth. They wear a purple sash with a gold D.

Berachiel – "*Blessings of God*" – Head of the Dominions, also head of the guardian angels of nations and people.

Gagiel – Angel of waters and fish.

VIRTUES

Virtues are angels who personify a given quality. They wear a white sash with a gold V.

Eleleth – The Angel of Peace, who becomes sick as the war in Heaven drags on.

Abbadon – Friend of Eleleth who turns into the Demon of War, becoming stronger even as Eleleth fades.

Numinel – The Angel of Knowledge, subordinate of Gabriel.

Zadkiel – *"Righteousness of God"* - The Angel of Mercy.

Verin – Angel who later becomes the Demon of Impatience.

Dahaka – Angel who later becomes the Demon of Doubt and Confusion.

Bushyasta – Demon of Laziness, lulls people to sleep when they try to pray.

Asmodeus – Angel who later becomes the Demon of Lust.

Zebub/Baalzebub – Angel who leads the first rebellion against God. Later becomes the Demon of Pride. Lucifer changes his name to call him Lord Zebub.

Belial – Angel who later becomes the Demon of Worthlessness

POWERS

Powers are warrior angels who are in charge of the defense of Heaven.

Azazel – The head of the Powers who is chief in charge of the defense of Heaven. Later a demon who specializes in teaching humans the use of deadly weapons and subterfuge. His chief nemesis is Raphael.

Verchiel – Lieutenant of Azazel who later becomes head of the Powers. He is also in charge of training and tactics.

Raguel – "*Friend of God*" – Angel of justice.

Eligos – Power who falls and later becomes a demon who knows the future of wars and rides on a winged horse.

Cantos – Desk keeper of the armory. He is the first angel slain and sent to the Containment.

PRINCIPALITIES

Principalities are in charge of 100 angels. They wear white sashes with a blue P.

Uriel – "*Light of God*" – Kind, gentle angel who serves as Alizel's Principality.

Kasadya – Calm, even and rational, Kasadya is the angel who later becomes the demon in charge of child sacrifices and abortion. He is unable to appreciate miracles, especially the miracle of new life.

Oliver – Double agent for Gabriel whose use of hate leaves him caught between the two sides.

ARCHANGELS

Archangels are responsible for looking after a group of ten angels. They wear white sashes with a green A.

Katel – Alizel's archangel, sent to the Containment in the war.

UNRANKED

The lowest order of angels wear grey sashes with no letter.

Alizel – Main character, narrator of the Angel Wars saga.

Semyaza – Angel awed at the beauty of human females.

Cimeriel – "*Darkness of God*" later turns to Kimaris. Warrior on a black horse. Can locate hidden things and treasures.

Gylou – Woman who causes miscarriage or other childbirth ailments. Subordinate of Kasadya.

Hyveriel – Honey colored skin and sapphire blue feathers. Unranked friend of Alizel.

Mupiel – Blond Unranked friend of Alizel who is very curious about everything.